ELIZABET
GASKEL
FOUR
SHORT STORIES

Elizabeth Gaskell née Stevenson was born in Chelsea in 1810. Elizabeth was thirteen months old when her mother died, and she was taken to Knutsford in Cheshire to be brought up by an aunt. She had the benefit of a liberal education with the Misses Byerley at Stratford and left school in 1827. In 1832 she married a Unitarian minister, William Gaskell, and they went to live in Manchester, an environment to which she never really adapted. The Gaskells had four daughters and a son who died when he was a year old. Elizabeth Gaskell's life was a very active one. She not only ran a home and brought up her daughters, but gave considerable help to her husband in his parish affairs.

In addition to all this, her output of novels, among them *Cranford, Ruth* and *Wives and Daughters,* and short stories was considerable.

Her writing often paid for extras in the family life-style, including trips abroad with one or more of her daughters. Elizabeth Gaskell died suddenly in 1865, having just negotiated the purchase of a new family home in Alton, Hampshire.

Anna Walters studied English as a mature student at Bedford College, University of London, graduating in 1969. She explored Elizabeth Gaskell's treatment of her heroines in her MA thesis, written whilst she worked as Head of the Department of English at a large comprehensive school. Now a business executive, Anna Walters continues to write in her spare time.

ELIZABETH GASKELL

FOUR SHORT STORIES

THE THREE ERAS OF LIBBIE MARSH
LIZZIE LEIGH
THE WELL OF PEN-MORFA
THE MANCHESTER MARRIAGE

INTRODUCED BY ANNA WALTERS

PANDORA PRESS

Routledge & Kegan Paul
London, Boston, Melbourne and Henley

This collection first published in 1983
by Pandora Press (Routledge & Kegan Paul plc)
39 Store Street, London WC1E 7DD,
9 Park Street, Boston, Mass. 02108, USA,
296 Beaconsfield Parade, Middle Park,
Melbourne, 3206, Australia and
Broadway House, Newtown Road,
Henley-on-Thames, Oxon RG9 1EN
Photoset in 10 on 11½pt Garamond by
Kelly Typesetting Ltd, Bradford-on-Avon, Wiltshire
and printed in Great Britain by
Redwood Burn Ltd, Trowbridge, Wiltshire

Library of Congress Cataloging in Publication Data

Gaskell, Elizabeth Cleghorn, 1810–1865.
Selected short stories.

Contents: The three eras of Libbie Marsh – Lizzie
Leigh – The well of Pen-Morfa – [etc.]
I. Walters, Anna. II. Title.
PR4710.A4 1983   823'.8   82–22289

ISBN 0–86358–001–7

CONTENTS

INTRODUCTION

Until the last decade Elizabeth Gaskell was known as the writer of *Cranford*, which, although a little masterpiece of its kind, is hardly representative of her as a writer. It is gradually becoming recognized that Gaskell was at the forefront of those nineteenth-century writers who used the novel as a medium to criticize the social institutions of their age. It is perhaps less well known that she extended this criticism into her writing of short stories, but the four stories in this volume are clear evidence of this. It is also interesting to note that stories such as these would escape the critical censure which Gaskell's novels received. Published in various journals over the years, they were an excellent medium through which Gaskell could explore often quite radical ideas without drawing the spotlight of critical attention upon herself. The publication of a short story was inevitably less of an event than that of a novel, but it is clear that the concerns of some of the stories in this volume are those very concerns which Gaskell was to develop at greater length in her novels.

When the first story in this collection, *The Three Eras of Libbie Marsh*, was published in 1847, Elizabeth had been married to William Gaskell, a Unitarian minister, for fifteen years, and a great deal had happened in that time. At this date Elizabeth was the mother of four daughters, but she had also lost a cherished baby son, William, at the age of ten months. This loss had a profound effect upon Elizabeth and the deep grief it caused left a residue of morbidity which sometimes makes itself evident in her writing. It was to deflect her from dwelling on this loss that her husband encouraged her to begin writing seriously. Husband and wife had already published a piece of writing, *Sketches among the Poor*, in *Blackwood's Magazine* and had collaborated in other ventures, such as preparing a series of lectures on Wordsworth and Coleridge for the Mechanics Institute where William lectured. They had a great many interests in common, not the least of these being their mutual involvement in the social problems which William encountered in his work as a minister in the poorer districts of Manchester. It seems clear that Elizabeth's most natural response to these problems was to work them through imaginatively in writing and it is very probable that she had been trying her hand at short stories for several years before the publication of *Libbie Marsh*.

The Gaskells were friends of William and Mary Howitt, a husband and wife team who wrote articles for literary journals. Elizabeth had been in contact with Mary Howitt since 1838, in fact it was the Howitts who probably opened Elizabeth's eyes to the possibility of writing professionally. When the Howitts launched their literary weekly for a shilling a copy in 1847, Elizabeth contributed three stories to it, of which *The Three Eras of Libbie Marsh* was the first. *Howitt's Journal* was aimed at a working-class public and contained both educational and instructional material as well as what was considered to be improving literature. Elizabeth Gaskell's humanitarian approach was particularly appropriate to such a journal, but unfortunately the workers themselves preferred to be entertained rather than educated and the journal failed after a year. *The Three Eras of Libbie Marsh* also disappeared practically without trace, which was a loss, because apart from being a moving tale in its own right, it revealed in embryo some of the major concerns which were to occupy Gaskell throughout her career as a writer. These issues upon which she chose to focus her attention were not typical of those usually to be found in mid-nineteenth-century literature, but Elizabeth Gaskell was far from being a typical mid-nineteenth-century woman.

In the first place it was not usual for a woman to be writing at all. We perhaps tend to forget just how much a woman writer offended the social norm as we complacently survey the literary greats of the nineteenth century. We forget the climate of opinion, against which, in adopting their male pseudonyms, they hoped to protect themselves. When Mary Ann Evans published *Adam Bede* under the pseudonym of George Eliot, the man with whom she lived, who happened to be an eminent literary critic, declared, 'It is quite clear that people would have sniffed at it if they had known the writer to be a woman but they cannot now unsay their admiration.'[1]

Many people are now familiar with Southey's notorious response to Charlotte Brontë on the subject of women becoming writers. Our familiarity with his utterance perhaps lessens our ability to empathize with Charlotte Brontë's feelings when she read it. 'Literature cannot be the business of a woman's life and it ought not to be. The more she is engaged in her proper duties the less leisure will she have for it, even as an accomplishment and a recreation.'[2] It took considerable conviction to begin writing in such a climate of opinion and temerity indeed to attempt publication.

Like the Brontë's and Eliot, Gaskell published at first under a pseudonym. Her short stories in *Howitt's Journal* were attributed to Cotton Mather Mills, whilst her first novel, *Mary Barton*, was published anonymously in 1848. It is fascinating to discern the changed tone of the critics when they discovered *Mary Barton* to be the work of a woman.

Elizabeth Gaskell was not without her own conflicts over what Southey described as a woman's 'proper duties'. She pursued her roles as wife and mother whilst continuing her writing at the same time. She wrote in the dining room, which had three doors leading out of it from which she supervised the household. That this arrangement could lead to conflict is evidenced in a letter to one of her male friends:

If I had a library like yours all undisturbed for hours how I would write! Mrs. Chapone's letters should be nothing to mine! I would outdo *Rasselas* in fiction. But you see everybody comes to me perpetually. Now in this hour since breakfast I have had to decide on the following variety of important questions. Boiled beef – how to boil? What perennials will do in Manchester smoke, and what colours our garden wants. Length of skirt for a gown. Salary of a nursery governess and stipulations for a certain quantity of time to be left to herself. Settle twenty questions of dress for the girls . . . and it's not half past ten yet.[3]

Clearly Elizabeth's domestic role often proved an obstacle to writing. In addition the subjects which interested her as a writer were not subjects to which the Victorian literary public were accustomed. The public was addicted to novels about high society. Harriet Martineau had difficulties publishing *Deerbrook* in 1848, because her hero was middle-class rather than aristocratic, he was a surgeon and came from Birmingham! In 1846 Charlotte Brontë met with a similar problem when trying to publish *The Professor*, because she emphasized her hero's need to earn a living. Yet in Gaskell's novels and stories not only are her characters often working-class but additionally the economic realities of their lives are prime motivators in the narrative. Her first novel, *Mary Barton*, published in 1848, caused a furore in Parliament, so powerful was its description of the plight of the mill hands in Manchester. Members of her husband's congregation burned her second novel, *Ruth*, published in 1853, because its heroine was an unmarried mother.

Indeed women are often Gaskell's chief protagonists and frequently they are not portrayed in any significant relationship with men. They exist in their own right. Libbie Marsh, the heroine of the first story in this collection, is not a wife, a mother, a sister or a fiancée. In most Victorian fiction she would be invisible. The concerns of a little seamstress in a working-class district of Manchester were not the stuff of which fiction was usually made.

There were strict rules about literary heroines, which Elizabeth Gaskell ignored from the outset. The mainstream of fiction in the 1840s served to strengthen the ramparts of the Victorian view of woman's role. It emphasized the vital part woman played in supporting the institution of marriage by subordinating her personality to that of the male. She might learn as much as would be amenable to him in having his views understood and supported. Marriage was the core of social life, the only desirable goal for a woman. The following lines from a very popular novelist of the time, Geraldine Jewsbury, encapsulate the ideal heroine. 'Kate needed to be loved, protected, guided. Her intelligent passivity was to Charles an intense attraction, her noble nature seemed to fertilize under his culture.'[4]

Young heroines in novels prepared themselves to enter into the happy state these lines describe by looking lovely and being helpless. Independent action, assertiveness, high spirits and any attempt at serious thought were activities subversive to the social framework. There is no doubt that Elizabeth Gaskell was fully aware of the demands of the stereotype, but perhaps because she was daily observing four girls growing up and because her integrity of observation made it impossible for her to collude with the myths of the feminine, she chose to break the rules and describe girls and women as she saw them. Whatever the cause, she often takes an opportunity to satirize the literary heroine, as in the following description of Edith, the girl Gaskell does *not* choose for her heroine in *North and South*!

Edith had fallen asleep. She lay curled up on the sofa in the back drawing-room in Harley Street, looking very lovely in her white muslins and blue ribbons. If Titania had ever dressed in white muslins and blue ribbons, and had fallen asleep on a crimson damask sofa in a back drawing-room, Edith might have been taken for her.[5]

Gaskell was never really interested in girls like Edith. Some of her heroines are actually plain, all are spirited and capable of independent action. Of the girls in the following stories only one is married; she is Alice in *The Manchester Marriage*, and in this story there is an exploration of a dynamic interaction between the sexes in which the man stands to gain. It is also Alice's second marriage and she has had a period of independence between the two. The other three heroines are single. Libbie earns her own living and chooses to live in a mutually supportive relationship with another woman. Lizzie in *Lizzie Leigh* has an illegitimate child and becomes a prostitute to support it. Nest Gwyn in *The Well of Pen-Morfa* is betrayed by her lover when she becomes a cripple. All these situations are at a far remove from the orthodox plot of Victorian fiction, in which the reader could enjoy watching the heroine pursue her path to matrimony with a few setbacks on the way to add zest to the narrative. Not only does Gaskell choose to place her heroines in unorthodox situations but, in apparently inconsequential asides, she criticizes the institution of marriage. Cumulatively these asides form a powerful statement about the plight of women in the marriage market and the double standard of nineteenth-century society.

One of the most difficult things to decide about Elizabeth Gaskell is how far all this criticism of the norm was conscious on her part, or how far it was what some critics have described as the triumph of the unconscious. Her determination to break away from the cult of the conventional heroine was clearly a conscious decision, as she must have been made forcibly aware of the extent to which she was offending public taste by the degree of critical hostility which some of her heroines met with. When, for example, in 1863 Gaskell published *Sylvia's Lovers*, this was the reaction to the heroine on the part of the reviewer in the *Spectator*: 'She is hard selfish and unforgiving. . . . She is, to our judgement as bad a specimen of womanhood as we were ever asked to study and most unreal besides.'[6] So far removed is Sylvia from the model of womanhood with which the reviewer can cope, that his only resource is to insist that there is no truth in the portrait – it can't happen. In spite of the critics, however, Gaskell continued to create heroines of her own liking, culminating in Cynthia in *Wives and Daughters*, who speaks with the voice of the twentieth century.

It is much more difficult to decide the extent to which Gaskell intended to criticize the idealized model of marriage and to expose the double standards inherent in society's attitude towards the sexes. It may be that the full implications of some of her comments and observations were not apparent to her, and that she simply described the truth as she saw it without the conscious intention of subverting traditional views. Here is a typical exposure of the gap between image and truth of which she seemed so fond. The brother and sister in *Ruth* are walking to the Welsh village where Ruth lies ill. The nonsense of social appearance and the necessity of colluding with it is conveyed in an apparently irrelevant detail: 'She helped him with tender care and gave her arm up the long and tedious hill; but when they approached the village without speaking a word on the subject, they changed position and she leant (apparently) on him.'[7] Gaskell often shows a humorous awareness of the mutual co-existence of male and female qualities in both sexes and does not seem to have the need to polarize the sexes found in so many of her contemporaries: 'Miss Benson had some masculine tricks and one was whistling a long low whistle when surprised or displeased.'[8] In fact Faith Benson's gruff utterances are more reminiscent of a country squire than a minister's sister and are a perfect foil for her brother's gentle speculative consideration.

Whatever Elizabeth Gaskell's position in relation to 'the Woman Question', the publication of a novel like *Ruth* attracted the attention of those at the forefront of the movement to liberate women. The Swedish novelist Frederika Bremer, a pioneer of the movement, wrote to Gaskell in 1853 saying, 'Dear Elizabeth, dear sister in spirit, if I may call you so, give me your hand in sympathy and in work for the oppressed or neglected of our own sex.'[9]

There can be no doubt that Elizabeth Gaskell strove to help ameliorate the position of women in many undesirable circumstances. It was in fact in the course of eliciting Charles Dickens's help in the case of a young prostitute that Gaskell was invited to contribute a story to his journal *Household Words*. Dickens assured Gaskell that all contributions would be anonymous and added that the general objectives of his journal were humanitarian, 'the raising up of those that are down and the general improvement of our social condition'.[10] The story which Gaskell first sent to Dickens was *Lizzie Leigh*, the second in this volume. Dickens was so delighted with the story that he invited Gaskell to make further contributions, one of which was *The Well of Pen-Morfa*. In fact contributions to *Household Words* were to prove a lucrative source of income for Gaskell over the years. She frequently ran up short stories at considerable speed for Dickens in order to meet expenses such as those incurred on the trips abroad she took with her daughters. *The Manchester Marriage* was written in Heidelberg in 1858 in order to finance a trip to Dresden. Some of the questions raised in these stories, such as the shortcomings of the obedience model in marriage in *Lizzie Leigh* and the hypocrisy of the marriage market in *The Well of Pen-Morfa*, passed quietly unnoticed in these short stories, which did not have to meet the stringent censorship of the circulating libraries which was imposed on the novel.

The opening lines of *The Three Eras of Libbie Marsh* typify Gaskell's way of subverting traditional views. It is in the apparently insignificant phrase that we find so much of Gaskell's questioning of the establishment. Much will depend on the reader's selection, but cumulatively throughout her work these phrases can be seen to result in a powerful argument. In one brief aside Gaskell summarizes all that society felt/feels about women who have not achieved marital status. Their every action lacks significance. Nothing they do is imbued with the importance that it would have were it the action of a man. In the second sentence of this easy conversational opening this attitude is brilliantly exposed. There is no undue emphasis, merely a casual remark, 'hardly a flitting after all, for it was *only a single person changing her place of abode*'.[11]

In Gaskell's novels and stories, unlike most of the writing of her time, women are not always seen in relation to men. The Victorian patriarchal pyramid is in fact noticeably absent from this short story. *The Three Eras of Libbie Marsh* is about working women and how they survive without men. Indeed the two glances at marriage in the story are not a recommendation for that institution, but are a salutary reminder of how the ralities of the way people live affect the quality of their relating. When Libbie reflects on her parents' past marriage she remembers drunkenness and

infanticide: ' "Oh, Anne, God above only knows what the wife of
a drunken man has to bear. Don't tell," said she lowering her
voice, "but father killed our little baby in one of his bouts." ' [12] So
authentically have the living conditions of the poor been described
in the story, that it is difficult for the reader to impute blame. The
inference throughout is that it is the social circumstances giving
rise to such actions which must be changed. Anne Dixon's antici-
patory comments about her future married life suggest that her
chances of happiness are equally hazardous. She would rather
have her future husband tipsy than sober and he already feels that
she cannot make him a good wife as too much of her time is taken
up in the factory. Marrying for both of them is 'just a spree', an
attitude designed to horrify Gaskell's Victorian readers and to
force them to consider the circumstances which have produced it.
We are made to feel that Libbie's future as a single woman in a
mutually supportive relationship with Margaret Hall may well
have more to recommend it in terms of quality of living than Anne
Dixon's marriage. It would be false to suggest that Gaskell dis-
approved of matrimony; so many of her letters reveal the opposite. What is evident is her determination not to collude with the
myths of happy ever after, and her concern to show how social
and economic realities are inextricably linked with a potential for
human happiness. Very important also is her constant exploration
of models of relationship other than marriage which are accorded
significance and *stature*. Margaret Hall develops and changes
because of her relationship with Libbie. Theirs becomes a positive
and viable way of life, not a sad second best to marriage.

   It is interesting that in one of her first published stories Gaskell
insisted on making her heroine plain. Libbie had no hope of
performing a woman's 'dearest duties' in having a home of her
own to run. In thus placing her heroine outside the conventional
structure, Gaskell ran the risk of alienating her public at the
beginning of her tale. She has long been praised for her integrity of
observation and it is this quality which made it impossible for her
to write within the myth of being feminine. Gaskell wrote about
what she saw, and just as she saw the back-to-back terrace houses
in Manchester, so she saw the reality of being female in that
environment. It was probably not Gaskell's deliberate intention
to probe myths, but her honesty made it inevitable. Libbie Marsh
is realistically portrayed. We know how she earns her living, the
circumstances in which she lives, and have access to her inner

hopes and fears. There are none of the challenges and obstacles of courtship so dear to the readers of romance; rather our concern is for a young seamstress who buys a canary for a crippled boy, befriending him and his washerwoman mother. Not the stuff of which immortal literature is made, a critic might say, but then much the same was said about the subjects of Wordsworth's *Lyrical Ballads*. Gaskell has been described as the prose Wordsworth, and nowhere does she more ably demonstrate her affinities with the poet than in some of her short stories.

In *The Three Eras of Libbie Marsh* Gaskell relies upon a simple and moving tale to carry a variety of concerns beneath its surface; such is the naturalness of her prose and the power of her observation that the seemingly frail vehicle succeeds in so doing. *The Three Eras of Libbie Marsh* functions successfully as a tale, because the circumstance under which Franky supports his feeble little life are so authentically realized. It would be difficult to remain uninvolved with these characters who 'are elbowed by life at every turn'. It is rare to find in other literature of the time such *a felt sense* of the unremitting grind of working-class life, which does not even allow a time for mourning. 'And I mun go washing just as if nothing has happened,'[13] says Margaret, after Franky's funeral.

Yet, in spite of all the grimness, we are shown ways in which the people made life supportable. The purchase of Jupiter provides an opportunity for Gaskell to propound one of her favourite themes. Throughout industrial cities like Manchester were people quietly intent on pursuing interests involving a level of knowledge which would astound the more 'educated'. The man who sells the canary to Libbie is typical of such men:

> There are enthusiasts about all sorts of things, both good and bad; and many of the weavers of Manchester know and care more about birds than any one would easily credit. Stubborn, silent, reserved men on many things, you have only to touch on the subject of birds to light up their faces with brightness.[14]

Working with her husband in the slums of Manchester served to reinforce Gaskell's belief in the regenerative powers of nature, and Franky's simple day excursion in this short story is developed into a major theme. The trip to Dunham Woods is fully orchestrated in both major and minor keys; the whole movement dominated by one theme 'this lapping the soul in green images of the country'.

Gaskell's faith in the beauty of nature to restore people to their
better selves and to reinstate a feeling of harmony, community,
co-operation and wholeness, is nowhere more lyrically stated
than in this second part of *Libbie Marsh*. As they return to the city
the workers

> turned backwards to cast a longing lingering look at Dunham
> Woods, fast deepening into the blackness of night, but whose
> memory was to haunt in greenness and freshness many a
> loom and workshop and factory with images of peace and
> beauty.[15]

It is the same feeling which informs Alice's description of her
childhood in *Mary Barton*, as she sits in her damp cellar in a dark
street and remembers

> Gray pieces o'stone as large as a house, all covered over wi'
> moss of different colours, some yellow, some brown, and the
> ground beneath them knee-deep in purple heather, smelling
> sae sweet and fragrant, and the low music of the humming bee
> for ever sounding among it.[16]

Gaskell is often accused of morbidity, yet Franky's death is
handled with restraint. There is no undue lingering at the grave,
but rather a concern with how those remaining pursue their lives.
Even within the space of the short story a dynamic relationship
between Libbie and Margaret is established and we are left with a
sense of growth and development rather than one of stasis.

Lizzie Leigh, published in *Household Words* in 1850, both
looks back to *Mary Barton* and forward to *Ruth* in terms of its
main concerns. In the character of Esther in *Mary Barton* Gaskell
had achieved a wholly convincing picture of the path to prostitution. If women aspired to better things the only ladder of promo-
tion was through the male, and the necessary qualifications were
physical. It was unfortunately impossible to be a self-made
woman. Esther aspires and is, of course, betrayed. She wants to
get away from the sweat shops and the slums and for three years
she does so. She dares to say that she would not take back those
three years with her lover, even though when he leaves her there
are few courses open to her as a 'fallen woman'. Her plight is seen
as pitiful rather than shameful. In *Ruth* the double standards
applied to illegitimacy were to be quite ruthlessly exposed. Ruth's
lover pays for his peccadillo with £50, Ruth pays eventually with
her life. It took considerable courage to publish novels on such
subjects in the mid-nineteenth century as was made evident in

their critical reception. A well-known writer and critic of the time, Mrs Oliphant, considered *Ruth* 'a great blunder in art' and declaimed at length on the mistake of choosing such a heroine at all.

It would seem that Gaskell's refusal to be influenced by convention sprang from the force of her real-life experiences. It was her work among prostitutes which led her to question the double standards of her society, and even though *Ruth* was to be burned by members of her husband's congregation, the sincerity of her feelings in writing it convinced others of its value. The experiences which motivated Gaskell to explore such themes in fiction are well documented in her letters. In January 1850 she wrote the following to Dickens:

> I am just now very much interested in a young girl, who is in our New Bayley prison. . . . When she was about 14, she was apprenticed to an Irish dress-maker here, of very great reputation for fashion. Last September but one this dress-maker failed, and had to dismiss all her apprentices; she placed this girl with a woman who occasionally worked for her, and who has since succeeded to her business; this woman was very profligate and connived at the girl's seduction *by a surgeon in the neighbourhood who was called in when the poor creature was ill*. Then she was in despair and wrote to her mother (who had never corresponded with her all the time she was at school and as apprentice) and while waiting the answer went into the penitentiary; she wrote 3 times but no answer came, and in desperation she listened to a woman, who had obtained admittance to the penitentiary solely as it turned out to decoy girls into her mode of life, and left with her, and for four months she has led the most miserable life.[17]

The emphasis is mine. Gaskell does not comment on the character of the surgeon, her feelings on the matter are written into the characterization of Bellingham in *Ruth*.

Lizzie Leigh appeared in March of the same year, and in that month the girl who is the subject of the above letter sailed for a new life in a new country. Her plight clearly prompted Gaskell into the appeal for Christian charity which is the central theme of *Lizzie Leigh*.

The frustration of battering against a rigid patriarchal order in *Lizzie Leigh* makes itself forcibly felt from the story's inception.

Within a few paragraphs we are aware of the whole conflict and are made to feel the stern, unbending character of the dead husband. Even more we are impressed with the wife's frustrated rebellion in acquiescing to his wishes. The prison constructed for women in the words 'to love, honour and obey' is powerfully conveyed. This is Gaskell's first attack on the obedience model in marriage and it is woven centrally into her tale. Had Mrs Leigh followed her own judgment Lizzie would have been rescued from prostitution; indeed Lizzie would never have gone to the city alone in the first place. Compassion, warmth, loyalty, love and tolerance are the province of the women in this tale, who in terms of humanity stand head and shoulders above their male partners. Will, the elder son, has inherited much of his father's inflexible character, but is influenced by the loving generous spirit of Susan Palmer.

Gaskell takes great care to define the traditional structure of Christian marriage before using the rest of her tale to indicate its shortcomings:

> They had been two-and-twenty years man and wife; for
> nineteen of those years their life had been as calm and happy,
> as the most perfect uprightness on the one side, and the most
> complete confidence and loving submission on the other,
> could make it. Milton's famous line might have been framed
> and hung up as the rule of their married life, for he was truly
> the interpreter, who stood between God and her.[18]

It is very apparent in this story that Gaskell believes women equally able to interpret God's will in their own right. Sometimes she dares to suggest that they are better able to do so. This is a direct challenge to the existing social order. It could imply that women are equal partners in marriage which in turn would validate their judgments. Once widowed, Mrs Leigh is free to dictate her own actions, and shows a remarkable singularity of purpose for one who has been accustomed to a submissive role all her life. Her motivating force is her love for her daughter Lizzie, and it is this relationship which dominates the tale. Mrs Leigh organizes the letting of the farm and the move to Manchester. It is love which gives her the spirit and conviction to persuade Will that the move is necessary and also gives her the strength to roam the streets of Manchester at night looking for her lost daughter. In matters which concern her children Mrs Leigh can find both courage and endurance. It is with attention to the smallest of details that Gaskell achieves some of her most memorable moments; one such is Mrs Leigh's donning of the scarlet cloak to face Susan Palmer with the truth about Lizzie.

Once again Gaskell has created in Susan Palmer a portrait of a young girl obviously at odds with conventional expectations. Susan's beauty is within not without. She is one of the many women characters through whom Gaskell seems determined to undermine the importance which society places upon image. Susan supports herself and an errant tippling father through her teaching. She does not subordinate her wishes to those of Will's in the way that Mrs Leigh did to Will's father. The reader can only feel thankful that the fates of Lizzie and her child are in Susan's hands not Will's, because her humanity dwarfs that of her future husband. She has a larger spirit. As in the case of many of Shakespeare's couples, we feel the man to be unworthy of his future wife, although guided by her he may begin to develop some stature. Susan is capable of some very direct utterance which invites Will's response 'Thou has spoke out very plain to me', yet at the end of this particular conversation Susan has resorted to 'sweet confusion' and we are approaching the stereotype once more. So much of Gaskell's writing is characterized by this method of pushing at the frontiers of acceptability and retiring just short of a radical statement. Susan must defer to Will. We are left, however, with the impression that the marriage between Susan and Will will be far more one of equals than that of the Leighs and, more importantly, that it is the male who will have to develop to become worthy of his female. As the end of the story approaches Will is already developing into a far more sympathetic character, a person who is open to change: 'and at first I could not feel all at once as thou wouldst have me. But I'm not cruel and hard.'[19]

At the level of plot as well as that of characterization Gaskell has to compromise with the establishment. It was not possible to write a completely happy ending for *Lizzie Leigh*; retribution for Lizzie's sin must be made and the child is made the sacrifice. The modern reader may well find this irritating, but viewed in relation to the age in which it was written, it is more surprising that Gaskell dared such a subject at all than that she compromised with a dominant ideology. Will voices the opinion of the times when he finds it difficult to understand how Susan could have dealings with Lizzie's baby, sullied as it must be by the circumstances of its birth. Will learns to feel differently because of his love for Susan and it is clearly Gaskell's belief that in such feeling lies the best hope for change. Her plea is for compassion, but beneath the surface clearly articulated is anger with a society which inhibits women from helping each other, so enthralled are they by man-made rules contrived to protect man's best interests. Throughout the action of the story, men impede the women's compassionate actions and it is Susan's father who indirectly causes the baby's death. In showing Susan Palmer in a supportive relationship with Lizzie, a role which may well have alienated her future husband, Gaskell is indicating the possibility of a support system which could go some way to counteract the injustice inherent in the social situation. If that situation is to change, the story suggests that it is the women who must change it and to do so may well involve breaking their vow of obedience in marriage.

The Well of Pen-Morfa, also published in 1850, later in the year, shows a continuing concern with the plight of women seduced and betrayed. Although the substance of the main tale is not concerned with seduction, the opening account of the woman and her illegitimate child provides an important image for the tale proper. That image is one of vulnerability, alienation and loneliness; it is also one of self-sufficiency, endurance, loyalty and love. This woman has returned to Pen-Morfa to rear her crippled child alone. Gaskell's determination to point out the frequency of illegitimacy, an aspect of life which the Victorians would choose to ignore, is clear. The impact of one action upon the whole course of this woman's life is also insisted upon. 'I dare say the story is common enough. . . . One event had made her savage and distrustful to her kind.'[20] The woman is betrayed and lonely but the picture that remains in the reader's mind is one of activity and independence. When we meet her she is 'hiving a swarm of bees alone and unassisted'. The verisimilitude of the opening passage, which gives the impression of turning the pages of an old diary, lends complete authenticity to the scene. Typically, Gaskell has made it very clear how this particular person survives. The economic basis of her life is clarified; like Susan Dixon in *Half a Life Time Ago*, who runs a farm unaided, this woman survives in the circumstances in which she finds herself. We are left as so often in Gaskell's writing with the impression of what women *can* do rather than the reverse. The woman's abiding love for her child evidently gives her the courage to continue this lonely existence. As in *Lizzie Leigh* love between mother and daughter is also the most important emotion in *The Well of Pen-Morfa*. In the main tale there is a romance vital to the narrative and a perceptive study of the emotions of an adolescent girl, but it is the love of Eleanor Gwynn for her beautiful young daughter upon which the story centres.

Nest Gwynn's tragedy enables Gaskell to trace the development of some complex feelings in her heroine. Her theme, as in much of her writing, is redemption through suffering, but it is difficult to see in what way Nest is culpable in the first place, her only adolescent 'sin' being her high spirits and a touch of vanity. It is interesting to speculate that after the death of her baby son Willie, the apparent injustice of suffering may well have been the subject of much of Gaskell's thoughts. She certainly had to wrestle with despair after this event, in much the same way that Nest has to cope with an overwhelming bitterness in the tale.

Nest's youthful ebullience and beauty are matched by the glory of the Welsh landscape, indeed in the opening of the main tale Gaskell rivals the Brontës in her descriptive powers. The impression of a young girl's reactions to her first love has the impact of a real understanding and sexuality is not evaded. 'She danced and sang more than ever; and then sat silent, and smiled to herself; if spoken to, she started and came back to the present with a scarlet blush, which told what she had been thinking of.'[21]

Vigour and vitality characterize all that Nest does. In the early part of the tale she closely resembles Sylvia in *Sylvia's Lovers*, who also was to have those high spirits dimmed in a different kind of prison. The path from adolescence to womanhood in Gaskell's women characters is worth attention. All the girls have to suffer a diminution of their powers in order to qualify for womanhood. Nest's case is exceptionally tragic. Crippled for life, she is deserted by her farmer lover: 'her disabled frame was a disqualification for her ever becoming a farmer's wife.'[22] It is difficult to feel that this is anything other than a convenient rationalization on Edward's part, even when taking into consideration Gaskell's view of marriage as an economic reality as well as a union of feeling. Edward's response in this tale is permeated with the callousness of the market place. Nest is a damaged object; she has lost her sale's value and therefore has lost the privilege of acquiring so desirable a protector. The physical attributes which Edward valued at the beginning of the tale were associated with her beauty, not her ability to cart water. It is only when Nest loses the qualities which

Edward really desired that he suddenly becomes aware of the more practical disadvantages in marrying a cripple.

Nest's mother is the focus of interest through much of the tale and like Mrs Leigh she finds courage and outspokenness when it comes to the defence of her child. In the scene between the mother and the erstwhile suitor there is no doubt where Gaskell's sympathy lies. What is selected out as important is the courage that Eleanor Gwynn has to find even to approach this young lord of creation. He holds every advantage and Mrs Gwynn knows the rules. Her anger at Edward's neglect must not be shown. She must attempt to avoid confrontation. It is only Edward's revealing assessment of Nest's present chances in the marriage market, his suggestion that she may still succeed in attracting a suitor with less expectations than he, that finally provokes the mother into direct confrontation.

' – unless indeed she could catch Mr Griffiths of
Tynwntyrybwlch; he might keep her a carriage, may-be.'
Edward really did not mean to be unfeeling. . . .

'Put it in words like a man. . . .'

'I cannot – no one would expect me to wed a cripple.'[23]
Although reduced to begging, the mother emerges as immeasurably the stronger of the two human beings. Her patience, courage and endurance are shown in marked contrast to Edward's self-interest.

Once again, Gaskell has placed her heroine outside the conventional structure of society to fend for herself and to battle with despair. It is Nest's inner struggle and the relationship between mother and daughter which must now interest the reader. It is only at the death of her mother that Nest is shaken out of bitterness and despair to take any positive action. Her solution in adopting the poor half-wit at least enables her to make an active contribution to life.

The only sympathetic male character in this collection of stories makes his appearance in *The Manchester Marriage* in the person of Mr Openshaw and he is an excellent example of Gaskell's approach to maledom. Her vision of the male is the product of an essentially female perspective, and as such seldom satisfies the expectations of male critics. Gaskell tends gently to undermine the importance of many of her male characters by pointing with unerring skill to their little whims and foibles. Her capacity for detailed observation is at its best in some of these portraits. The men emerge as powerful children, seen from this female point of view. Their power, of course, lies in the weight patriarchal society attributes to their judgments, rather than in their inherent wisdom. As we have already seen in *Lizzie Leigh*, Gaskell often implies that these judgments are faulty and can result in tragedy. It is a theme she pursues at greater length in several of her novels.

The tone of the opening of *The Manchester Marriage* is mildly satirical both in terms of the attitude of North towards South and in terms of marriage. The mood of the whole is one of self-satisfied complacency. Mr Openshaw leads an ordered life and his marriage is a paradigm of societal values. 'His wife was a pretty, gentle woman, of suitable age and character. He was forty-two, she thirty-five. He was loud and decided; she soft and yielding.'[24]

As soon as we turn to Alice's story we make contact with the reality of emotions which lies beneath such smooth surface definitions. Alice experiences two courtships and two marriages in the tale. The first courtship is allowed little space but within it Gaskell manages to convey Alice's sexual hesitancy and Frank's callow enthusiasm, whilst providing a motivation for the marriage that bears no relation to established myths:

So when her cousin, Frank Wilson, came home from a long absence at sea, and first was kind and protective to her; secondly, attentive; and thirdly, desperately in love with her, she hardly knew how to be grateful enough to him. It is true, she would have preferred his remaining in the first or second stages of behaviour; for his violent love puzzled and frightened her.[25]

It is unusual to find so overt an exploration of the incompatibility which can lie beneath the surface of youthful sexual relationships, particularly when that exploration shows the reality of a young girl's feelings. It is also not the stuff of romance to insist on so realistic a motive for entering into matrimony. Alice marries her cousin to escape from her aunt: 'At length she went to such extremes of crossness that Alice was only too glad to shut her eyes and rush blindly at the chance of escape from domestic tyranny offered her by a marriage with her cousin.'[26]

Alice's second courtship has the stamp of a mutually advantageous business arrangement and is conducted in humorous vein. Alice has three minutes to decide whether she will 'put up her horses' with Mr Openshaw and her reason for acceptance is the love of her child: 'If you please, sir – you have been so good to little Ailsie.' Gaskell has already provided the reader with the exact nature of Alice's financial predicament. The boarding house which she is running with Mrs Wilson and Norah is beginning to fail when Mr Openshaw becomes their lodger. The women are surviving alone, but only barely. In Mr Openshaw's offer lies permanent protection from such struggle and every advantage for the child. Alice enters into this marriage with much the same feeling that one signs a contract for a good steady job; it may not be wildly exciting but it is sensible to take it. Her 'wild deep passionate affection' is reserved for her child.

Mr Openshaw's reasons are equally practical. He has been well serviced by Alice and this, in his opinion, is the highest possible recommendation for marital felicity:

But, when he found out the punctuality with which his wishes were attended to, and her work was done; when he was called in the morning at the very stroke of the clock, his shaving-water scalding hot, his fire bright, his coffee made exactly as his peculiar fancy dictated (for he was a man who had his theory about everything based upon what he knew of science, and often perfectly original) – then he began to think; not that Alice had any particular merit, but that he had got into remarkably good lodgings.[27]

The tone here is one of shrewd indulgence towards the male which encompasses a knowledge of their little whims and fancies certain to detract from any suggestion of superiority. It is in this tone of mild amusement and semi-condescension that Gaskell describes so many of her male characters. Whether her conscious intention was to indulge in a little debunking is irrelevant; what happens is that the patriarch is portrayed without his pedestal. What happens also is that we are made to realize the chasm which separates male and female in terms of their potential for determining the course of their lives. For in this courtship scene between Alice and Mr Openshaw we have the typical picture of woman powerless and vulnerable through the presence of a child and man powerful and magnanimous. Mr Openshaw commends Alice's good sense in accepting his offer. Her refusal could only have indicated a failure in her judgment and *given the circumstances* which Gaskell has been at pains to elaborate, the reader can only agree. It is the sensible thing to do. He holds all the cards. ' "There, sit down comfortably by me on the sofa, and let's have our tea together. I am glad to find you are as good and sensible as I took you for." And this was Alice Wilson's second wooing.'[28] On the surface of things Mr Openshaw carries all before him, in the public sphere his is the power, but Gaskell uses the rest of the story to show what he has to gain as a human being from his contact with the women in the story. At the opening of the tale, he is the Victorian examplar of the self-made man, a vehicle for satire; at the end he is an admirable human being. This development is achieved through his ability to learn and to adopt the female perspective into his scheme of things. In this story it is the man who, at the human level, has everything to gain from the marriage contract.

At the opening of the story he is perilously near being a mere cog in the Victorian commercial system: 'I do not think he ever saw a group of flowers in the fields without thinking whether their colour would, or would not, form harmonious contrasts in the coming spring muslins and prints.'[29]

The tenderness and compassion inherent in his character are almost submerged by the demands of his upward social mobility, until initially Ailsie and eventually Alice enable him to respond at a feeling level. It is in the conflict caused by Frank's return, however, that Mr Openshaw emerges at his most sympathetic. In the debate about the theft of the brooch he has the clear choice of appearing to be lord and master in his own home, or of making concessions to his wife's feelings, and he chooses the latter. It is at that point in the story that he escapes from the cosy confines of his male role into the hardship of thinking as a person, and he is perplexed.

Mr Openshaw's initial appraisal of the situation concerning Norah, the unknown man and the stolen brooch, springs from the certain assumption that the mainspring of Norah's action must lie in her need for the opposite sex. This in his view is so natural and inevitable that he is willing to be very generous in his responses towards her:

'Now, my notion is, that this Norah of ours has been come
over by some good-for-nothing chap (for she's at the time o'
life when they say women pray for husbands – "any, good
Lord, any") and has let him into our house.'[30]

At the moment in the story when Norah's capacity for independent action and inner strength, inspired by her love for her mistress, are clearly emphasized, Mr Openshaw is generously condescending to her frailty as a woman:

'and you've been just like all other women, and have turned a

soft place in your heart to him; and he came last night
a-lovyering, and you had him up in the nursery, and he made
use of his opportunities, and made off with a few things on his
way down!'[31]

This is indeed the conventional picture of woman used and
abused, and Norah is quick to recognize the tone of pity and
condescension extended to any woman who, having failed to
catch a husband, must be desperate for any male attention: 'You
may ask that question, and taunt me with my being single.'[32]

Everyone in the story, except Alice, finds this sexual motivation
for Norah's behaviour instantly credible, including the police. It
fits perfectly with their perceptions of the world. When Norah
voices her feelings for Alice to Mr Openshaw he cannot recognize
the significance of the outburst, it is outside his scheme of refer-
ence. He is, however, influenced by the unexpected passion with
which Alice defends Norah to the Chadwicks.

Openshaw's gentleness and compassion towards Norah when
he finds her near the end of the story are all the more commend-
able as he does not yet know the secret which she is hiding. When
he learns her story, his distress and instant sympathy for Frank's
plight combine with the quality of resolution which he has always
possessed to produce the best possible response to a tragic situation. What can be retrieved from the tragedy in terms of a caring
response is accomplished by Mr Openshaw. Norah is sent home
to Alice and the practicalities surrounding Frank's death are dealt
with. Alice is protected from a great deal of pain by her husband,
but it is through her in the first place that he has learned the
compassion and consideration which enable him to act in the way
he does. It is a neat reversal of the traditional pattern to observe a
man learning new behaviour patterns through his contact with a
household of women.

Gaskell, perhaps unwittingly, reveals the model of the suc-
cessful business man as a depleted one, a model to be mildly
disdained, unless it can be seen to include qualities which relate to
a larger apprehension of life. It is the feeling-based value system of
the women which emerges in this story as fundamentally worth-
while and it is to this that the man must cede if he is to become a
whole person.

It is difficult not to surmise that the central concerns of these
stories have remained inconspicuous to generations of critics who
have given them brief mention. On reflection this is not sur-

prising. To date most critics have been male. The male critic will select out for approval writing which most ably articulates experience as he perceives it. Much of the experience described in these short stories will appear trivial and insignificant to males and this will result in the undervaluing of the writing. Virginia Woolf saw all this very clearly in 1928:

> It is probable, however, that both in life and in art the values of a woman are not the values of a man. Thus, when a woman comes to write a novel, she will find that she is perpetually wishing to alter the established values – *to make serious what appears insignificant to a man, and trivial what is to him important*.[33]

I have emphasized the last part of Woolf's discussion because it would seem to me to summarize precisely what Gaskell does throughout all her writing and would certainly largely account for the fact that these stories have received so little attention.

Some of the dilemmas posed in these stories in relation to woman's role in society have certainly not yet been solved. This makes them both exciting and relevant for the modern reader, whose awareness of the problems articulated in the stories will be heightened by all that has contributed to twentieth-century consciousness. The stories still constitute a challenge to established values, a challenge which may well be more fully perceived by a modern reader than her Victorian counterpart. The frontiers which Gaskell delineates were still undefined as frontiers by most Victorians. For many modern readers the frontiers are clear. The problem lies in crossing them.

To select a model for living other than that of wife and mother still involves loss of status, both economic and social, for a woman. Only a privileged minority are exempt from this. It remains a problem for a girl to be pregnant and unmarried. It is extremely difficult to be a single parent. It invites speculation to remain unmarried even when pursuing a prestigious career. It is a work of art *really* to remain an equal partner within matrimony. It is often necessary to justify a decision to remain childless. Anything other than the established norm of husband, wife and 2.4 children will still necessitate explanation or be perceived as a failure to achieve the ideal. It is challenging to discover that more than a century ago a minister's wife with four children was insisting on the *positive* possibility of other alternatives.

Anna Walters

REFERENCES

1 Stern, Jenny, 1972, 'Women and the Novel', *Women's Liberation Review*, Falling Wall Press.

2 Gaskell, E., 1857, *Life of Charlotte Brontë*; Penguin edn, 1975.

3 Chapple, J. A. V. and Pollard, A., 1966, *The Letters of Mrs Gaskell*, Manchester University Press, no. 61.

4 Jewsbury, Geraldine, 1855, *Constance Herbert*, vol. 1, ch. 4.

5 Gaskell, E., 1855, *North and South*; Penguin edn, 1970.

6 *Spectator*, Review, 1863, *Sylvia's Lovers*.

7 Gaskell, E., 1853, *Ruth*; Everyman edn, 1974.

8 Op. cit.

9 Rubenius, Aina, 1950, *The Woman Question in Mrs Gaskell's Life and Works*, Harvard University Press.

10 Dexter, W., 1938, *The Letters of Charles Dickens*, vol. 11.

11 Gaskell, E., *The Three Eras of Libbie Marsh*, *Howitt's Journal*, vol. 1, London, 1847, my emphasis.

12 Op. cit.

13 Op. cit.

14 Op. cit.

15 Op. cit.

16 Gaskell, E., *Mary Barton*, London, Penguin edn, 1976, p. 70.

17 Chapple, J. A. V. and Pollard, A., 1966, *The Letters of Mrs Gaskell*, Manchester University Press, no. 61.

18 Gaskell, E., *Lizzie Leigh*, London, *Household Words*, vol. 1, 1850.

19 Op. cit.

20 Gaskell, E., *The Well of Pen-Morfa*, London, *Household Words*, vol. 11, 1850.

21 Op. cit.

22 Op. cit.

23 Op. cit.

24 Gaskell, E., *The Manchester Marriage*, London, *Household Words*, 1858.

25 Op. cit.

26 Op. cit.

27 Op. cit.

28 Op. cit.

29 Op. cit.

30 Op. cit.

31 Op. cit.

32 Op. cit.

33 Woolf, V., 1929, 'Women and Fiction', *Forum*, London, March.

THE THREE ERAS OF LIBBIE MARSH

ST VALENTINE'S DAY

Last November but one there was a flitting in our neighbourhood; hardly a flitting after all, for it was only a single person changing her place of abode, from one lodging to another; and instead of a comfortable cartload of drawers, and baskets, and dressers, and beds, with old king clock at the top of all, there was only one large wooden chest to be carried after the girl, who moved slowly and heavily along the streets, listless and depressed more from the state of her mind than of her body. It was Libbie Marsh, who had been obliged to quit her room in Dunn Street, because the acquaintances, with whom she had been living there, were leaving Manchester. She tried to think herself fortunate in having met with lodgings rather more out of the town, and with those who were known to be respectable; she did indeed try to be contented, but in spite of her reason, the old feeling of desolation came over her, as she was now about to be again thrown entirely among strangers.

No. 2, —— Court, Albemarle Street, was reached at last; and the pace, slow as it was, slackened, as she drew near the spot where she was to be left by the man who carried her box; for trivial as his acquaintance with her was, he was not quite a stranger, as every one else was, peering out of their open doors, and satisfying themselves it was only 'Dixon's new lodger.'

Dixon's house was the last on the left hand side of the court. A high dead brick wall connected it with its opposite neighbour. All the dwellings were of the same monotonous pattern, and one side of the court looked at its exact likeness opposite, as if it were seeing itself in a looking-glass.

Dixon's house was shut up, and the key left next door; but the woman in whose care it was knew that Libbie was expected, and came forwards to say a few explanatory words, to unlock the door, and stir the dull-grey ashes which were lazily burning in the

23

grate, and then she returned to her own house; leaving poor Libbie standing alone with her great big chest on the middle of the house-place floor, with no one to say a word, (even a common-place remark would have been better than that dull silence), that could help her to repel the fast-coming tears.

Dixon and his wife, and their eldest girl, worked in factories and were absent all day from their house; the youngest child, (also a little girl), was boarded out for the week days at the neighbour's where the door-key was deposited; but, although busy making dirt-pies at the entrance to the court when Libbie came in, she was too young to care much about her parents' new lodger. Libbie knew she was to sleep with the elder girl in the front bed-room; but, as you may fancy, it seemed a liberty even to go up stairs to take off her things, when no one was at home to marshal the way up the ladder-like steps. So she could only take off her bonnet, and sit down, and gaze at the now blazing fire, and think sadly on the past, and on the lonely creature she was in this wide world.

Father and mother gone; her little brother long since dead; (he would have been more than nineteen, had he been alive, but she only thought of him as the darling baby); her only friends (to call friends) living far away at their new home; her employers, – kind enough people in their way, but too rapidly twirling round on this bustling earth to have leisure to think of the little work-woman, excepting when they wanted gowns turned, carpets mended, or household linen darned; and hardly even the natural, though hidden hope, of a young girl's heart, to cheer her on with bright visions of a home of her own at some future day, where, loving and beloved, she might fulfil a woman's dearest duties.

For Libbie was very plain, as she had known so long, that the consciousness of it had ceased to mortify her. You can hardly live in Manchester without having some idea of your personal appearance. The factory lads and lasses take good care of that, and if you meet them at the hours when they are pouring out of the mills, you are sure to hear a good number of truths, some of them combined with such a spirit of impudent fun, that you can scarcely keep from laughing even at the joke against yourself. Libbie had often and often been greeted by such questions as 'How long is it since you were a beauty?' 'What would you take a day to stand in a field to scare away the birds?' etc., for her to linger under any delusion as to her looks.

While she was thus musing, and quietly crying over the pictures her fancy conjured up, the Dixons came dropping in, and surprised her with wet cheeks and quivering lips.

She almost wished to have the stillness again she had felt so oppressive an hour ago, they talked and laughed so loudly and so much, and bustled about so noisily over every thing they did. Dixon took hold of one iron handle of her box, and helped her to bump it up stairs; while his daughter Anne followed to see the unpacking, and what sort of clothes 'little sewing-body had gotten.' Mrs Dixon rattled out the tea-things, and put the kettle on; fetched home her youngest child, which added to the commotion. Then she called Anne down stairs and sent her off for this thing, and that. Eggs to put to the cream, it was so thin. Ham to give a relish to the bread and butter. Some new bread (hot, if she could get it). Libbie heard all these orders given at full pitch of Mrs Dixon's voice, and wondered at their extravagance, so different to the habits of the place where she had last lodged. But they were fine spinners in the receipt of good wages; and confined all day to an atmosphere ranging from 75 to 80 degrees; they had lost all natural healthy appetite for simple food, and having no higher tastes, found their greatest enjoyment in their luxurious meals.

When tea was ready, Libbie was called down stairs with a rough but hearty invitation to share their meal; she sat mutely at the corner of the tea-table, while they went on with their own conversation about people and things she knew nothing about; till at length she ventured to ask for a candle to go and finish her unpacking before bed-time, as she had to go out sewing for several succeeding days. But once in the comparative peace of her bedroom her energy failed her, and she contented herself with locking her Noah's ark of a chest, and put out her candle, and went to sit by the window and gaze out at the night heavens; for ever and ever the 'blue sky that bends over all,' sheds down a feeling of sympathy with the sorrowful at the solemn hours, when the ceaseless stars are seen to pace its depths.

By and by her eye fell down to gazing at the corresponding window to her own on the opposite side of the court. It was lighted, but the blind was drawn down. Upon the blind she saw, at first unconsciously, the constant weary motion of a little, spectral shadow; a child's hand and arm, – no more; long, thin fingers hanging listlessly down from the wrist, while the arm moved up and down, as if keeping time to the heavy pulses of dull pain. She could not help hoping that sleep would soon come to still that incessant, feeble motion; and now and then it did cease, as if the little creature had dropped into a slumber from very weariness; but presently the arm jerked up with the fingers clenched, as if with a sudden start of agony. When Anne came up to bed, Libbie was still sitting watching the shadow; and she directly asked to whom it belonged.

'It will be Margaret Hall's lad. Last summer when it was so hot, there was no biding with the window shut at nights; and their'n were open too; and many's the time he waked me up with his moans. They say he's been better sin' cold weather came.'

'Is he always so bad? Whatten ails him?' asked Libbie.

'Summut's amiss wi' his back-bone, folks say; he's better and worse like. He's a nice little chap enough; and his mother's not that bad either; only my mother and her had words, so now we don't speak.'

Libbie went on watching, and when she next spoke to ask who and what his mother was, Anne Dixon was fast asleep.

Time passed away, and, as usual, unveiled the hidden things.

Libbie found out that Margaret Hall was a widow, who earned her living as a washerwoman; that this little suffering lad was her only child, her dearly beloved. That while she scolded pretty nearly every body else 'till her name was up' in the neighbourhood for a termagant, to him she was evidently most tender and gentle. He lay alone on his little bed near the window through the day, while she was away, toiling for a livelihood. But when Libbie had plain sewing to do at her lodgings instead of going out to sew, she used to watch from her bed-room window for the time when the shadows opposite, by their mute gestures, told that the mother had returned to bend over her child; to smooth his pillow, to alter his position, to get him his nightly cup of tea. And often in the night Libbie could not help rising gently from bed to see if the little arm was waving up and down, as was his accustomed habit when sleepless from pain.

Libbie had a good deal of sewing to do at home that winter, and whenever it was not so cold as to numb her fingers, she took it up stairs in order to watch the little lad in her few odd moments of pause. On his better days he could sit up enough to peep out of his window, and she found he liked to look at her. Presently she ventured to nod to him across the court, and his faint smile, and ready nod back again, showed that this gave him pleasure. I think she would have been encouraged by this smile to proceed to a speaking acquaintance, if it had not been for his terrible mother, to whom it seemed to be irritation enough to know that Libbie was a lodger at the Dixons', for her to talk *at* her whenever they encountered each other, and to live evidently in wait for some good opportunity of abuse.

With her constant interest in him, Libbie soon discovered his great want of an object on which to occupy his thoughts, and which might distract his attention, when alone through the long day, from the pain he endured. He was very fond of flowers. It was November when she had first removed to her lodgings, but it had been very mild weather and a few flowers yet lingered in the gardens, which the country-people gathered into nosegays, and brought on market days into Manchester. His mother had bought him a bunch of Michaelmas daisies the very day that Libbie had become a neighbour, and she watched their history. He put them first in an old tea-pot, of which the spout was broken off, and the lid lost; and he daily replenished the tea-pot from the jug of water his mother left near him to quench his feverish thirst. By and by one or two out of the constellation of lilac stars faded, and then the time he had hitherto spent in admiring (almost caressing) them, was devoted to cutting off those flowers whose decay marred the beauty of his nosegay. It took him half the morning with his feeble languid motions, and his cumbrous old scissors, to trim up his diminishing darlings. Then at last he seemed to think he had better preserve the few that remained by drying them; so they were carefully put between the leaves of the old Bible; and then whenever a better day came, when he had strength enough to lift the ponderous book, he used to open its pages to look at his flower friends. In winter he could have no more living flowers to tend.

Libbie thought and thought, till at last an idea flashed upon her mind that often made a happy smile steal over her face as she stitched away, and which cheered her through that solitary winter – for solitary it continued to be, although the Dixons were very good sort of people; never pressed her for payment if she had had but little work that week; never grudged her a share of their extravagant meals, which were far more luxurious than she could have met with any where else for her previously agreed payment in case of working at home; and they would fain have taught her to drink rum in her tea, assuring her that she should have it for nothing, and welcome. But they were too loud, too prosperous, too much absorbed in themselves to take off Libbie's feeling of solitariness; not half as much as did the little face by day, and the shadow by night, of him with whom she had never yet exchanged a word.

Her idea was this: her mother came from the east of England, where, as perhaps you know, they have the pretty custom of sending presents on St Valentine's day, with the donor's name unknown, and of course that mystery constitutes half the enjoyment. The 14th of February was Libbie's birthday too; and many a year in the happy days of old had her mother delighted to surprise her with some little gift, of which she more than half guessed the giver, although each Valentine's day the manner of its arrival was varied. Since then, the 14th of February had been the dreariest day of all the year, because the most haunted by memory of departed happiness. But now, this year, if she could not have the old gladness of heart herself, she would try and brighten the life of another. She would save, and she would screw, but she would buy a canary and a cage for that poor little laddie opposite, who wore out his monotonous life with so few pleasures, and so much pain.

I doubt I may not tell you here of the anxieties, and the fears, of the hopes, and the self-sacrifices, – all perhaps small in tangible effect as the widow's mite, yet not the less marked by the viewless angels who go about continually among us, – which varied Libbie's life before she accomplished her purpose. It is enough to say, it was accomplished. The very day before the 14th she found time to go with her half-guinea to a barber's, who lived near Albemarle Street, and who was famous for his stock of singing birds. There are enthusiasts about all sorts of things, both good and bad; and many of the weavers in Manchester know and care more about birds that any one would easily credit. Stubborn, silent, reserved men on many things, you have only to touch on the subject of birds to light up their faces with brightness. They will tell you who won the prizes at the last canary show, where the prize birds may be seen; and give you all the details of those funny though pretty and interesting mimicries of great people's cattle shows. Among these amateurs, Emanuel Morris the barber was an oracle.

He took Libbie into his little back room, used for private shaving of modest men, who did not care to be exhibited in the front shop, decked out in the full glories of lather; and which was hung round with birds in rude wicker cages, with the exception of those who had won prizes, and were consequently honoured with gilt wire prisons. The longer and thinner the body of the bird was, the more admiration it received as far as its external beauty went; and when in addition to this chance the colour was deep and clear, and its notes strong and varied, the more did Emanuel dwell upon their perfections. But these were all prize birds; and on inquiry Libbie heard, with a little sinking at her heart, that their price ran from one to two guineas.

'I'm not over-particular as to shape and colour,' said she. 'I should like a good singer, that's all.'

She dropped a little in Emanuel's estimation. However, he showed her his good singers, but all were above Libbie's means.

'After all, I don't think I care so much about the singing very loud, it's but a noise after all; and sometimes noises fidgets folks.'

'They must be nesh folk as is put out with the singing o' birds,' replied Emanuel, rather affronted.

'It's for one who is poorly,' said Libbie, deprecatingly.

'Well,' said he, as if considering the matter, 'folk that are cranky often take more to them as shows 'em love, than to them who is clever and gifted. Happen yo'd rather have this'n,' opening a cage-door, and calling to a dull-coloured bird, sitting moped up in a corner, 'Here! Jupiter, Jupiter!'

The bird smoothed its feathers in an instant, and uttering a little note of delight, flew to Emanuel, putting its beak to his lips as if kissing him, and then perching on his head, it began a gurgling warble of pleasure, not by any means so varied or so clear as the song of the others, but which pleased Libbie more (for she was always one to find out she liked the gooseberries that were accessible, better than the grapes which were beyond her reach). The price, too, was just right; so she gladly took possession of the cage, and hid it under her cloak, preparatory to carrying it home. Emanuel meanwhile was giving her directions as to its food, with all the minuteness of one loving his subject.

'Will it soon get to know any one?' asked she.

'Give him two days only, and you and he'll be as thick as him and me are now. You've only to open his door, and call him, and he'd follow you round the room; but he'd first kiss you, and then perch on your head. He only wants larning, (which I've no time to give him), to do many another accomplishment.'

'What's his name? I didn't rightly catch it.'

'Jupiter; it's not common, but the town is o'errun with Bobbys and Dickys, and as my birds are thought a bit out o' the way, I like to have better names for 'em, so I just picked a few out o' my lad's school-books. It's just as ready, when you're used to it, to say Jupiter as Dicky.'

'I could bring my tongue round to Peter better; would he answer to Peter?' asked Libbie, now on the point of departure.

'Happen he might; but I think he'd come readier to the three syllables.'

On Valentine's day, Jupiter's cage was decked round with ivy leaves, making quite a pretty wreath on the wicker-work; and to one of them was pinned a slip of paper, with these words written in Libbie's best round hand: –

'From your faithful Valentine. Please take notice: His name is Peter, and he will come if you call him, after a bit.'

But little work did Libbie do that afternoon, she was so engaged in watching for the messenger who was to bear her present to her little Valentine, and run away as soon as he had delivered up the canary, and explained for whom it was sent.

At last he came, then there was a pause before the woman of the house was at leisure to take it up stairs. Then Libbie saw the little face flush into a bright colour, the feeble hands tremble with delighted eagerness, the head bent down to try and make out the writing, (beyond his power, poor lad, to read), the rapturous turning round of the cage in order to see the canary in every point of view, head, tail, wings and feet; an intention which Jupiter, in his uneasiness at being again among strangers, did not second, for he hopped round so as continually to present a full front to the boy. It was a source of never-wearying delight to the little fellow till daylight closed in; he evidently forgot to wonder who had sent it him, in his gladness at the possession of such a treasure; and when the shadow of his mother darkened on the blind, and the bird had been exhibited, Libbie saw her do what, with all her tenderness, seemed rarely to have entered into her thoughts – she bent down, and kissed her boy in a mother's sympathy with the joy of her child.

The canary was placed for the night between the little bed and window, and when Libbie rose once to take her accustomed peep, she saw the little arm put fondly round the cage, as if embracing his new treasure even in his sleep. How Jupiter slept that first night is quite another thing.

So ended the first day of Libbie's three eras in last year.

WHITSUNTIDE

The brightest, fullest daylight poured down into No. 2, ——
Court, Albemarle Street, and the heat, even at the early hour of
five, was almost as great as at the noontide on the June days of
many years past.

The court seemed alive, and merry with voices and laughter.
The bed-room windows were open wide, (and had been so all
night on account of the heat), and every now and then you might
see a head and a pair of shoulders, simply encased in shirt sleeves,
popped out, and you might hear the inquiry passed from one to
the other: –

'Well, Jack, and where art thou bound to?'

'Dunham!'

'Why what an old-fashioned chap thou be'st. Thy grandad
afore thee went to Dunham; but thou wert always a slow coach.
I'm off to Alderley, – me, and my missus.'

'Aye, that's because there's only thee and thy missus; wait
till thou hast getten four childer like me, and thou'lt be glad
enough to take 'em to Dunham, oud-fashioned way, for four-
pence a-piece.'

'I'd still go to Alderley; I'd not be bothered with my childer;
they should keep house at home.'

A pair of hands (the person to whom they belonged invisible
behind her husband) boxed his ears at this last speech, in a very
spirited, although a playful manner, and the neighbours all
laughed at the surprized look of the speaker, at this assault from an
unseen foe; the man who had been holding the conversation with
him, cried out,

'Sarved him right, Mrs Slater; he knows nought about it yet, but
when he gets them, he'll be as loth to leave the babbies at home on
a Whitsuntide, as any on us. We shall live to see him in Dunham
park yet, wi' twins in his arms, and another pair on 'em clutching
at daddy's coat tails, let alone your share of youngsters, missus.'

At this moment our friend Libbie appeared at her window, and
Mrs Slater, who had taken her discomfited husband's place, called
out,

'Elizabeth Marsh, where are Dixons and you bound to?'

'Dixons are not up yet; he said last night he'd take his holiday
out in lying in bed. I'm going to th' old-fashioned place, –
Dunham.'

'Thou art never going by thyself, moping!'

'No! I'm going with Margaret Hall and her lad,' replied Libbie, hastily withdrawing from the window in order to avoid hearing any remarks on the associates she had chosen for her day of pleasure – the scold of the neighbourhood, and her sickly, ailing child!

But Jupiter might have been a dove, and his ivy-leaves an olive-branch, for the peace he had brought, the happiness he had caused, to three individuals at least. For of course it could not long be a mystery who had sent little Frank Hall his Valentine; nor could his mother long maintain her hard manner towards one who had given her child a new pleasure. She was shy, and she was proud, and for some time she struggled against the natural desire of manifesting her gratitude; but one evening, when Libbie was returning home with a bundle of work half as large as herself, as she dragged herself along through the heated street she was over-taken by Margaret Hall, her burden gently pulled from her, and her way home shortened, and her weary spirits soothed and cheered by the outpourings of Margaret's heart; for her barrier of reserve once broken down, she had much to say, to thank her for days of amusement and happy employment for her lad, to speak of his gratitude, to tell of her hopes and fears – the hopes and fears which made up the dates of her life. From that time Libbie lost her awe of the termagant in interest for the mother, whose all was ventured in so frail a bark. From that time Libbie was a fast friend with both mother and son; planning mitigations to the sorrowful days of the latter, as eagerly as poor Margaret Hall, and with far more resources. His life had flickered up under the charm and the excitement of the last few months. He even seemed strong enough to undertake the journey to Dunham, which Libbie had arranged as a Whitsuntide treat, and for which she and his mother had been hoarding up for several weeks. The canal-boat left Knott-Mill at six, and it was now past five; so Libbie let herself out very gently, and went across to her friends. She knocked at the door of their lodging room, and without waiting for an answer entered.

Franky's face was flushed, and he was trembling with excite-ment, partly from pleasure, but partly from some eager wish not yet granted.

'He wants sore to take Peter with him,' said his mother, as if referring the matter to Libbie. The boy looked imploringly at her.

'He would so like it, I know. For one thing, he'd miss me sadly, and chirp for me all day long, he'd be so lonely. I could not be half so happy, a-thinking on him, left alone here by himself. Then Libbie, he's just like a Christian, so fond of flowers, and green leaves, and them sort of things. He chirrups to me so when mother brings me a pennyworth of wall-flowers to put round his cage. He would talk if he could, you know, but I can tell what he means quite as one as if he spoke. Do let Peter go, Libbie! I'll carry him in my own arms.'

So Jupiter was allowed to be of the party. Now Libbie had overcome the great difficulty of conveying Franky to the boat by offering to 'slay' for a coach, and the shouts and exclamations of the neighbours told them that their conveyance awaited them at the bottom of the court. His mother carried Franky, light in weight, though heavy in helplessness; and he would hold the cage, believing that he was thus redeeming his promise that Peter should be a trouble to no one. Libbie preceded to arrange the bundle containing their dinner, as a support in the corner of the coach. The neighbours came out with many blunt speeches, and more kindly wishes, and one or two of them would have relieved Margaret of her burden, if she would have allowed it. The presence of that little crippled fellow seemed to obliterate all the angry feelings which had existed between his mother and her neighbours, and which had formed the politics of that little court for many a day.

And now they were fairly off! Franky bit his lips in attempted endurance of the pain the motion caused him, but winced and shrunk, until they were fairly on a macadamized thoroughfare, when he closed his eyes, and seemed desirous of a few minutes' rest. Libbie felt very shy, and very much afraid of being seen by her employers 'set up in a coach;' and so she hid herself in a corner, and made herself as small as possible; while Mrs Hall had exactly the opposite feeling, and was delighted to stand up, stretching out of the window, and nodding to pretty nearly every one they met, or passed, on the footpaths; and they were not a few, for the streets were quite gay, even at that early hour, with parties going to this or that railway station; or to the boats which crowded the canals in this bright holiday week. And almost every one they met seemed to enter into Mrs Hall's exhilaration of feeling, and had a smile or a nod in return. At last she plumped down by Libbie and exclaimed,

'I never was in a coach but once afore, and that was when I was a going to be married. It's like heaven; and all done over with such beautiful gimp, too,' continued she, admiring the lining of the vehicle. Jupiter did not enjoy it so much.

As if the holiday time, the lovely weather, and the 'sweet hour of prime' had a genial influence, (as no doubt they have), everybody's heart seemed softened towards poor Franky. The driver lifted him out with the gentleness of strength, and bore him tenderly down to the boat; the people there made way, and gave him up the best seat in their power; or rather, I should call it a couch, for they saw he was weary, and insisted on his lying down – an attitude he would have been ashamed to assume without the protection of his mother and Libbie, who now appeared, bearing their tickets, and carrying Peter.

Away the boat went to make room for others; for every conveyance both by land and by water is in requisition in Whitsun-week to give the hard-worked crowds an opportunity of tasting the charms of the country. Even every standing place in the canal packets was occupied; and as they glided along, the banks were lined by people, who seemed to find it object enough to watch the boats go by, packed close and full with happy beings brimming with anticipation of a day's pleasure. The country through which they passed is as uninteresting as can well be imagined, but still it is country; and the screams of delight from the children, and the low laughs of pleasure from the parents, at every blossoming tree which trailed its wreaths against some cottage-wall, or at the tufts of late primroses which lingered in the cool depths of grass along the canal banks, the thorough relish of everything, as if dreading to let the least circumstance on this happy day pass over without its due appreciation, made the time seem all too short, although it took two hours to arrive at a place only eight miles distant from Manchester. Even Franky, with all his impatience to see Dunham woods, (which I think he confused with London, believing both to be paved with gold), enjoyed the easy motion of the boat as much, floating along, while pictures moved before him, that he regretted when the time came for landing among the soft green meadows that come sloping down to the dancing water's brim. His fellow passengers carried him to the park, and refused all payment; although his mother had laid by sixpence on purpose, as a recompense for this service.

'Oh, Libbie, how beautiful! Oh, mother, mother! Is the whole world out of Manchester as beautiful as this! I did not know trees were like this. Such green homes for birds! Look, Peter! would not you like to be there, up among those boughs? But I can't let you go, you know, because you're my little bird-brother, and I should be quite lost without you.'

They spread a shawl upon the fine mossy turf at the root of a beech tree, which made a sort of natural couch, and there they laid him, and bade him rest in spite of the delight which made him believe himself capable of any exertion. Where he lay, (always holding Jupiter's cage, and often talking to him as to a play-fellow), he was on the verge of a green area shut in by magnificent trees, in all the glory of their early foliage before the summer heats have deepened their verdure into one rich monotonous tint. And hither came party after party; old men and maidens, young men and children – whole families trooped along after the guiding fathers, who bore the youngest in their arms, or astride upon their backs, while they turned round occasionally to the wives, with whom they shared some fond local remembrance. For years has Dunham park been the favourite resort of the Manchester work-people; for more years than I can tell; probably ever since 'The Duke,' by his canals, opened out the system of cheap travelling. It is scenery, too, which presents such a complete contrast to the whirl and turmoil of Manchester; so thoroughly woodland, with its ancestral trees, (here and there lightning-blanched), its 'verdurous walls,' its grassy walks leading far away into some glade where you start at the rabbit, rustling among the last year's fern, and where the wood-pigeon's call seems the only fitting and accordant sound. Depend upon it, this complete sylvan repose, this accessible depth of quiet, this lapping the soul in green images of the country, forms the most complete contrast to a towns-person, and consequently has over such the greatest power to charm.

Presently Libbie found out she was very hungry. Now they were but provided with dinner, which was of course to be eaten as near twelve o'clock as might be; and Margaret Hall, in her prudence, asked a working man near, to tell her what o'clock it was?

'Nay!' said he; 'I'll ne'er look at clock or watch to-day. I'll not spoil my pleasure by finding out how fast it's going away. If thou'rt hungry, eat. I make my own dinner hour, and I've eaten mine an hour ago.'

So they had their veal pies, and then found out it was only about half-past ten o'clock, by so many pleasurable events had that morning been marked. But such was their buoyancy of spirits that they only enjoyed their mistake, and joined in the general laugh against the man who had eaten his dinner somewhere about nine. He laughed most heartily of all, till suddenly stopping, he said,

'I must not go on at this rate; laughing gives me such an appetite.'

'Oh, if that's all,' said a merry-looking man, lying at full length, and crushing the fresh scent out of the grass, while two or three little children tumbled over him, and crept about him, as kittens or puppies frolic with their parents; 'if that's all, we'll have a subscription of eatables for them improvident folk as have eaten their dinner for their breakfast. Here's a sausage pasty and a handful of nuts for my share. Bring round a hat, Bob, and see what the company will give.'

Bob carried out the joke, much to little Franky's amusement, and no one was so churlish as to refuse, although the contributions varied from a peppermint drop up to a veal-pie, and a sausage pasty.

'It's a thriving trade,' said Bob, as he emptied his hatful of provisions on the grass by Libbie's side. 'Besides, it's tip-top too to live on the public. Hark! what is that?'

The laughter and the chat were suddenly hushed, and mothers told their little ones to listen, as far away in the distance, now sinking and falling, now swelling and clear, came a ringing peal of children's voices, blended together in one of those psalm tunes which we are all of us familiar with, and which bring to mind the old, old days when we, as wondering children, were first led to worship 'Our Father,' by those beloved ones who have since gone to the more perfect worship. Holy was that distant choral praise even to the most thoughtless; and when it in fact was ended, in the instant's pause during which the ear awaited the repetition of the air, they caught the noon-tide hum and buz of the myriads of insects, who danced away their lives in that glorious day; they heard the swaying of the mighty woods in the soft, yet resistless breeze; and then again once more burst forth the merry jests and the shouts of childhood; and again the elder ones resumed their happy talk, as they lay or sat 'under the greenwood tree.' Fresh parties came dropping in; some loaded with wild flowers, almost with branches of hawthorn indeed; while one or two had made prize of the earliest dog-roses, and had cast away campion, stitchwort, ragged robin, all, to keep the lady of the hedges from being obscured or hidden among the commonalty.

One after another drew near to Franky, and looked on with interest as he lay, sorting the flowers given to him. Happy parents stood by, with their household bands around them in health and comeliness, and felt the sad prophecy of those shrivelled limbs, those wasted fingers, those lamp-like eyes, with their bright dark lustre. His mother was too eagerly watching his happiness to read the meaning of the grave looks, but Libbie saw them, and understood them, and a chill shudder went through her even on that day, as she thought on the future.

'Aye! I thought we should give you a start!'

A start they did give, with their terrible slap on Libbie's back, as she sat, idly grouping flowers, and following out her sorrowful thoughts. It was the Dixons! Instead of keeping their holiday by lying in bed, they and their children had roused themselves, and had come by the omnibus to the nearest point. For an instant the meeting was an awkward one on account of the feud between Margaret Hall and Mrs Dixon; but there was no long resisting of kindly Mother Nature's soothings at that holiday time, and in that lovely tranquil spot; or if they could have been unheeded, the sight of Franky would have awed every angry feeling into rest, so changed was he since the Dixons had last seen him; since he had been the Puck, or Robin-goodfellow of the neighbourhood, whose marbles were always rolling themselves under people's feet, and whose top strings were always hanging in nooses to catch the unwary. Yes! he, the feeble, mild, almost girlish-looking lad, had once been a merry, happy rogue, and as such often cuffed by Mrs Dixon, the very Mrs Dixon who now stood gazing with the tears in her eyes. Could she, in sight of him, the changed, the fading, keep up a quarrel with his mother?

'How long hast thou been here?' asked Dixon.

'Welly on for all day,' answered Libbie.

'Hast never been to see the deer, or the king and queen oaks? Lord! how stupid!'

His wife pinched his arm, to remind him of Franky's helpless condition, which of course tethered the otherwise willing feet.

But Dixon had a remedy. He called Bob, and one or two others, and each taking a corner of the strong plaid shawl, they slung Franky as in a hammock, and thus carried him merrily along down the wood-paths, over the soft grassy turf, while the glimmering shine and shadow fell on his upturned face. The women walked behind, talking, loitering along, always in sight of the hammock, now picking up some green treasure from the ground, now catching at the low-hanging branches of the horse-chestnut. The soul grew much on that day, and in those woods, and all unconsciously, as souls do grow. They followed Franky's hammock-bearers up a grassy knoll, on the top of which stood a group of pine-trees, whose stems looked like dark red gold in the sunbeams. They had taken Franky there to show him Manchester, far away in the blue plain, against which the woodland foreground cut with a soft clear line. Far, far away in the distance on that flat plain you might see the motionless cloud of smoke hanging over a great town; and that was Manchester, old, ugly, smoky Manchester! dear, busy, earnest, working, noble Manchester; where their children had been born, (and perhaps where some lay buried), where their homes were, where God had cast their lives, and told them to work out their destiny.

'Hurrah for oud smoke-jack!' cried Bob, putting Franky softly down on the grass, before he whirled his hat round, preparatory for a cheer. 'Hurrah! hurrah!' from all the men.

'There's the rim of my hat lying like a quoit yonder,' observed Bob quietly, as he replaced his brimless hat on his head, with the gravity of a judge.

'Here's the Sunday-school childer a-coming to sit on this shady side, and have their buns and milk. Hark! they're singing the Infant School grace.'

They sat close at hand, so that Franky could hear the words they sang, in rings of children, making (in their gay summer prints, newly donned for that week) garlands of little faces, all happy and bright upon the green hill side. One little 'Dot' of a girl came shyly near Franky, whom she had long been watching, and threw her half bun at his side, and then ran away and hid herself, in very shame at the boldness of her own sweet impulse. She kept peeping behind her screen at Franky all the time; and he meanwhile was almost too much pleased and happy to eat: the world was so beautiful; and men, and women, and children, all so tender and kind; so softened, in fact, by the beauty of that earth; so unconsciously touched by the Spirit of Love which was the Creator of that lovely earth. But the day drew to an end; the heat declined; the birds once more began their warblings; the fresh scents again hung about plant, and tree, and grass, betokening the fragrant presence of the reviving dew; and – the boat time was near. As they trod the meadow path once more, they were joined by many a party they had encountered during the day, all abounding in happiness, all full of the day's adventures. Long-cherished quarrels had been forgotten, new friendships formed. Fresh tastes and higher delights had been imparted that day. We have all of us one look, now and then, called up by some noble or loving thought, (our highest on earth), which will be our likeness in Heaven. I can catch the glance on many a face; the glancing light of the cloud of glory from Heaven, 'which is our home.' That look was present on numbers of hard-worked, wrinkled countenances, as they turned backwards to cast a longing, lingering look at Dunham woods, fast deepening into the blackness of night, but whose memory was to haunt in greenness and freshness many a loom, and workshop, and factory, with images of peace and beauty.

That night, as Libbie lay awake, revolving the incidents of the day, she caught Franky's voice through the open windows. Instead of the frequent moan of pain, he was trying to recall the burden of one of the children's hymns: –

'Here we suffer grief and pain,
 Here we meet to part again,
    In Heaven we part no more.
       Oh! that will be joyful,' etc.

She recalled his question, his whispered question, to her in the happiest part of the day. He asked, 'Libbie, is Dunham like Heaven? The people here are as kind as angels; and I don't want Heaven to be more beautiful than this place. If you and mother would but die with me, I should like to die, and live always there.' She had checked him, for she had feared he was impious; but now the young child's craving for some definite idea of the land to which his inner wisdom told him he was hastening, had nothing in it wrong or even sorrowful, for

'In Heaven we part no more.'

MICHAELMAS

The church clocks had struck three; the crowds of gentlemen returning to business after their early dinners had disappeared within offices and warehouses; the streets were comparatively clear and quiet, and ladies were venturing to sally forth for their afternoon's shopping, and their afternoon calls.

Slowly, slowly along the streets, elbowed by life at every turn, a little funeral wound its quiet way. Four men bore along a child's coffin; two women, with bowed heads, followed meekly.

I need not tell you whose coffin it was, or who were these two mourners. All was now over with little Frank Hall; his romps, his games, his sickening, his suffering, his death. All was now over, but the Resurrection and the Life!

His mother walked as in a stupor. Could it be that he was dead? If he had been less of an object to her thoughts, less of a motive for her labours, she could sooner have realized it. As it was, she followed his poor, cast-off, worn-out body, as if she were borne along by some oppressive dream. If he were really dead, how could *she* be alive?

Libbie's mind was far less stunned, and consequently far more active than Margaret Hall's. Visions, as in a phantasmagoria, came rapidly passing before her, – recollections of the time (which seemed now so long ago) when the shadow of the feebly-waving arm first caught her attention; of the bright, strangely isolated day at Dunham Park, where the world had seemed so full of enjoyment, and beauty, and life; of the long-continued heat, through which poor Franky had panted his strength away in the little close room, where there was no escaping the hot rays of the afternoon sun; of the long nights, when his mother and she had watched by his side, as he moaned continually, whether awake or asleep; of the fevered moaning slumber of exhaustion; of the pitiful little self-upbraidings for his own impatience of suffering, (only impatience to his own eyes, – most true and holy patience in the sight of others); and then the fading away of life, the loss of power, the increased unconsciousness, the lovely look of angelic peace which followed the dark shadow on the countenance, – where was he – what was he now?

And so they laid him in his grave; and heard the solemn funeral words; but far off, in the distance – as if not addressed to them.

Margaret Hall bent over the grave to catch one last glance – she had not spoken, or sobbed, or done aught but shiver now and then, since the morning; but now her weight bore more heavily on Libbie's arm, and without sigh or sound she fell, an unconscious heap on the piled-up gravel. They helped Libbie to bring her round; but long after her half-opened eyes and altered breathings showed that her senses were restored, she lay, speechless and motionless, without attempting to rise from her strange bed, as if earth now contained nothing worth even that trifling exertion.

At last Libbie and she left that holy consecrated spot, and bent their steps back to the only place more consecrated still; where he had rendered up his spirit; and where memories of him haunted each common, rude piece of furniture that their eyes fell upon. As the woman of the house opened the door, she pulled Libbie on one side, and said,

'Anne Dixon has been across to see you; she wants to have a word with you.'

'I cannot go now,' replied Libbie, as she pushed hastily along in order to enter the room (*his* room), at the same time with the childless mother. For, as she anticipated, the sight of that empty spot, the glance at the uncurtained open window, letting in the fresh air, and the broad rejoicing light of day, where all had so long been darkened and subdued, unlocked the waters of the fountain, and long and shrill were the cries for her boy, that the poor woman uttered.

'Oh! dear Mrs Hall,; said Libbie, herself drenched in tears, 'do not take on so badly; I'm sure it would grieve *him* sore, if he was alive, – and you know he is, – Bible tells us so; and may be he's here, watching how we go on without him, and hoping we don't fret over-much.'

Mrs Hall's sobs grew worse, and more hysterical.

'Oh! listen!' said Libbie, once more struggling against her own increasing agitation. 'Listen! there's Peter chirping as he always does when he's put about, frightened like; and, you know, he that's gone could never abide to hear the canary chirp in that shrill way.'

Margaret Hall did check herself, and curb her expression of agony, in order not to frighten the little creature he had loved; and as her outward grief subsided, Libbie took up the old large Bible, which fell open at the never-failing comfort of the 14th chapter of St John's Gospel. How often those large family Bibles do fall open at that chapter! as if, unused in more joyous and prosperous times, the soul went home to its words of loving sympathy when weary and sorrowful, just as the little child seeks the tender comfort of its mother in all its griefs and cares.

And Margaret put back her wet, ruffled, grey hair from her heated, tear-stained, woeful face, and listened with such earnest eyes; trying to form some idea of the 'Father's House,' where her boy had gone to dwell.

They were interrupted by a low tap at the door. Libbie went.

'Anne Dixon has watched you home, and wants to have a word with you,' said the woman of the house in a whisper. Libbie went back, and closed the book with a word of explanation to Margaret Hall, and then ran down stairs to learn the reason of Anne's anxiety to see her.

'Oh, Libbie!' she burst out with, and then checking herself, into the remembrance of Libbie's last solemn duty; 'how's Margaret Hall? But of course, poor thing, she'll fret a bit at first; she'll be some time coming round, mother says, seeing it's as well that poor lad is taken; for he'd always ha' been a cripple, and a trouble to her – he was a fine lad once, too.'

She had come full of another and a different subject; but the sight of Libbie's sad weeping face, and the quiet subdued tone of her manner, made her feel it awkward to begin on any other theme than the one which filled up her companion's mind. To her last speech, Libbie answered sorrowfully,

'No doubt, Anne, it's ordered for the best; but oh! don't call him, don't think he could ever ha' been a trouble to his mother, though he were a cripple. She loved him all the more for each thing she had to do for him, – I'm sure I did.' Libbie cried a little behind her apron. Anne Dixon felt still more awkward at introducing her discordant subject.

'Well! – Flesh is grass, Bible says!' and having fulfilled the etiquette of quoting a text if possible, if not, of making a moral observation on the fleeting nature of earthly things, she thought she was at liberty to pass on to her real errand.

'You must not go on moping yourself, Libbie Marsh. What I wanted special for to see you this afternoon, was to tell you, you must come to my wedding to-morrow. Nancy Dawson has fallen sick, and there's none I should like to have bridesmaid in her place so well as you.'

'To-morrow! Oh, I cannot; indeed I cannot.'

'Why not?'

Libbie did not answer, and Anne Dixon grew impatient.

'Surely in the name o' goodness, you're never going to baulk yourself of a day's pleasure for the sake of yon little cripple that's dead and gone?'

'No, – it's not baulking myself of, – don't be angry. Anne

Dixon, with me please, but I don't think it would be pleasure to me – I don't feel as if I could enjoy it; thank you all the same, but I did love that little lad very dearly, – I did,' (sobbing a little), 'and I can't forget him, and make merry so soon.'

'Well, I never!' exclaimed Anne, almost angrily.

'Indeed, Anne, I feel your kindness, and you and Bob have my best wishes, – that's what you have, – but even if I went, I should be thinking all day of him, and of his poor, poor mother, and they say it's bad to think over-much on them that is dead, at a wedding!'

'Nonsense!' said Anne, 'I'll take the risk of the ill-luck. After all, what is marrying? just a spree, Bob says. He often says he does not think I shall make him a good wife, for I know nought about house-matters wi' working in a factory; but he says he'd rather be uneasy wi' me, than easy wi' any one else. There's love for you! And I tell him I'd rather have him tipsy than any one else sober.'

'Oh, Anne Dixon, hush! you don't know yet what it is to have a drunken husband! I have seen something of it; father used to get fuddled: and in the long run it killed mother, let alone – Oh, Anne, God above only knows what the wife of a drunken man has to bear. Don't tell,' said she, lowering her voice, 'but father killed our little baby in one of his bouts; mother never looked up again, nor father either, for that matter, only his was in a different way. Mother will have gotten to little Jeannie now, and they'll be so happy together, – and perhaps Franky too. Oh!' said she, recovering herself from her train of thought, 'never say aught lightly of the wife's lot whose husband is given to drink.'

'Dear! what a preachment! I tell you what, Libbie! you're as born an old maid as ever I saw. You'll never be married, to either drunken or sober.'

Libbie's face went rather red, but without losing its meek expression.

'I know that as well as you can tell me. And more reason, therefore, that as God has seen fit to keep me out o' woman's natural work, I should try and find work for myself. I mean,' said she, seeing Anne Dixon's puzzled look, 'that as I know I'm never like for to have a home of my own, or a husband, who would look to me to make all straight, or children to watch over and care for, all which I take to be woman's natural work, I must not lose time in fretting and fidgeting after marriage, but just look about me for somewhat else to do. I can see many a one misses it in this. They

will hanker after what is ne'er likely to be theirs, instead of facing
it out, and settling down to be old maids; and as old maids, just
looking round for the odd jobs God leaves in the world for such as
old maids to do, – there's plenty of such work, – and there's the
blessing of God on them as does it.' Libbie was almost out of
breath at this outpouring of what had long been her inner
thoughts.

'That's all very true, I make no doubt, for them as is to be old
maids; but as I'm not, (please God, to-morrow comes), you might
have spared your breath to cool your porridge. What I want to
know is, whether you'll be bridesmaid to-morrow or not. Come
now, do! it will do you good, after all your watching, and
working, and slaving yourself for that poor Franky Hall.'

'It was one of my odd jobs,' said Libbie, smiling, though her
eyes were brimming over with tears. 'But, dear Anne,' continued
she, recovering herself, 'I could not do it to-morrow; indeed I
could not!'

'And I can't wait,' said Anne Dixon, almost sulkily. 'Bob and I
put it off from to-day because of the funeral, and Bob had set his
heart on its being on Michaelmas-day; and mother says the goose
won't keep beyond to-morrow. Do come! father finds eatables,
and Bob finds drink, and we shall be so jolly! And after we've been
to church, we're to walk round the town in pairs; white satin
ribbon in our bonnets, and refreshment at any public-house we
like. Bob says. And after dinner, there's to be a dance. Don't be a
fool; you can do no good by staying. Margaret Hall will have to go
out washing, I'll be bound.'

'Yes! she must go to Mrs Wilkinson's, and for that matter I must
go working too. Mrs Williams has been after me to make her girl's
winter things ready; only I could not leave Franky, he clung so to
me.'

'Then you won't be bridesmaid! Is that your last word?'

'It is; you must not be angry with me, Anne Dixon,' said
Libbie, deprecatingly.

But Anne was gone without a reply.

With a heavy heart Libbie mounted the little staircase. For she
felt how ungracious her refusal of Anne's kindness must appear to
one, who understood so little the feelings which rendered her
acceptance of it a moral impossibility.

On opening the door, she saw Margaret Hall, with the Bible
open on the table before her. For she had puzzled out the place

where Libbie was reading, and with her finger under the line, was spelling out the words of consolation, piecing the syllables together aloud, with the earnest anxiety of comprehension with which a child first learns to read. So Libbie took the stool by her side, before she was aware that any one had entered the room.

'What did she want you for?' asked Margaret. 'But I can guess: she wanted you to be at th'wedding as is to come off this week, they say. Ay! they'll marry, and laugh, and dance, all as one as if my boy was alive,' said she, bitterly; 'well, he was neither kith nor kin of yours, so I maun try and be thankful for what you've done for him, and not wonder at your forgetting him afore he's well settled in his grave.'

'I never can forget him, and I'm not going to the wedding,' said Libbie, gently, for she understood the mother's jealousy of her dead child's claims.

'I must go work at Mrs Williams's to-morrow,' she said in explanation, for she was unwilling to boast of the tender fond regret which had been her principal motive for declining Anne's invitation.

'And I mun go washing, just as if nothing had happened,' sighed forth Mrs Hall. 'And I mun come home at night, and find his place empty, and all still where I used to be sure of hearing his voice, ere ever I got up the stair. No one will ever call me mother again!'

She fell a crying pitifully, and Libbie could not speak for her own emotion for some time. But during this silence she put the key stone in the arch of thoughts she had been building up for many days; and when Margaret was again calm in her sorrow, Libbie said, 'Mrs Hall, I should like – would you like me to come for to live here altogether?'

Margaret Hall looked up with a sudden light on her countenance, which encouraged Libbie to go on.

'I could sleep with you, and pay half, you know; and we should be together in the evenings, and her as was home first would watch for the other, – and' (dropping her voice) 'we could talk of him at nights, you know.'

She was going on, but Mrs Hall interrupted her.

'Oh! Libbie Marsh! and can you really think of coming to live wi' me! I should like it above – But no! it must not be; you've no notion on what a creature I am at times. More like a mad one, when I'm in a rage; and I can't keep it down. I seem to get out of bed wrong side in the morning, and I must have my passion out with the first person I meet. Why, Libbie,' said she, with a doleful look of agony on her face, 'I even used to fly out on him, poor sick lad as he was, and you may judge how little I can keep it down frae that. No! you must not come. I must live alone now,' sinking her voice into the low tones of despair. But Libbie's resolution was brave and strong:

'I'm not afraid,' said she, smiling. 'I know you better than you know yourself, Mrs Hall. I've seen you try of late to keep it down, when you've been boiling over, and I think you'll go on a-doing so. And at any rate, when you've had your fit out you're very kind; and I can forget if you have been a bit put out. But I'll try not to put you out. Do let me come; I think *he* would like us to keep together. I'll do my very best to make you comfortable.'

'It's me! It's me as will be making your life miserable with my temper, or else, God knows how my heart clings to you. You and me is folk alone in the world, for we both loved one who is dead, and who had none else to love him. If you will live with me, Libbie, I'll try as I never did afore, to be gentle and quiet-tempered. Oh! will you try me, Libbie Marsh?'

So, out of the little grave, there sprang a hope and a resolution, which made life an object to each of the two.

When Elizabeth Marsh returned home the next evening from her day's labours, Anne (Dixon no longer) crossed over, all in her bridal finery, to endeavour to induce her to join the dance going on in her father's house.

'Dear Anne! this is good of you, a-thinking of me to-night,' said Libbie, kissing her. 'And though I cannot come, (I've promised Mrs Hall to be with her), I shall think on you, and trust you'll be happy; I have got a little needle-case, I looked out for you, – stay, here it is -- I wish it were more, only –'

'Only – I know what – you've been a-spending all your money in nice things for poor Franky. Thou'rt a real good 'un, Libbie, and I'll keep your needle-book to my dying day, that I will.'

Seeing Anne in such a friendly mood emboldened Libbie to tell her of her change of place; of her intention of lodging hence-forward with Margaret Hall.

'Thou never will! Why, father and mother are as fond of thee as can be, – they'll lower thy rent, if that's what it is; and thou know'st they never grudge thee bit or drop. And Margaret Hall of all folk to lodge wi'! She's such a Tartar! Sooner than not have a quarrel, she'd fight right hand against left. Thou'lt have no peace of thy life. What on earth can make you think of such a thing, Libbie Marsh?'

'She'd be so lonely without me,' pleaded Libbie. 'I'm sure I could make her happier (even if she does scold me a bit now and then) then she'd be living alone. And I'm not afraid of her; and I mean to do my best not to vex her; and it will ease her heart, may be, to talk to me at times about Franky. I shall often see your father and mother, and I shall always thank them for their kindness to me. But they have you, and little Mary, and poor Mrs Hall has no one.'

Anne could only repeat 'Well! I never!' and hurry off to tell the news at home.

But Libbie was right. Margaret Hall is a different woman to the scold of the neighbourhood she once was; touched and softened by the two purifying angels, Sorrow and Love. And it is beautiful to see her affection, her reverence for Libbie Marsh. Her dead mother could hardly have cared for her more tenderly than does the hard-featured washerwoman, not long ago so fierce and un-womanly. Libbie herself has such peace shining on her counte-nance, as almost makes it beautiful, as she renders the services of a daughter to Franky's mother – no longer the desolate, lonely orphan, a stranger on the earth.

Do you ever read the moral concluding sentence of a story? I never do; but I once (in the year 1811, I think) heard of a deaf old lady living by herself, who did; and as she may have left some descendants with the same amiable peculiarity, I will put in for their benefit what I believe to be the secret of Libbie's peace of mind, the real reason why she no longer feels oppressed at her own loneliness in the world.

She has a purpose in life, and that purpose is a holy one.

LIZZIE LEIGH

CHAPTER I

When Death is present in a household on a Christmas Day, the very contrast between the time as it now is, and the day as it has often been, gives a poignancy to sorrow, – a more utter blankness to the desolation. James Leigh died just as the far-away bells of Rochdale Church were ringing for morning service on Christmas Day, 1836. A few minutes before his death, he opened his already glazing eyes, and made a sign to his wife, by the faint motion of his lips, that he had yet something to say. She stooped close down, and caught the broken whisper, 'I forgive her, Anne! May God forgive me.'

'Oh my love, my dear! only get well, and I will never cease showing my thanks for those words. May God in heaven bless thee for saying them. Thou'rt not so restless, my lad! may be – Oh God!'

For even while she spoke, he died.

They had been two-and-twenty years man and wife; for nineteen of those years their life had been as calm and happy, as the most perfect uprightness on the one side, and the most complete confidence and loving submission on the other, could make it. Milton's famous line might have been framed and hung up as the rule of their married life, for he was truly the interpreter, who stood between God and her; she would have considered herself wicked if she had ever dared even to think him austere, though as certainly as he was an upright man, so surely was he hard, stern, and inflexible. But for three years the moan and the murmur had never been out of her heart; she had rebelled against her husband as against a tyrant, with a hidden sullen rebellion, which tore up the old land-marks of wifely duty and affection, and poisoned the fountains whence gentlest love and reverence had once been for ever springing.

But those last blessed words replaced him on his throne in her heart, and called out penitent anguish for all the bitter estrangement of later years. It was this which made her refuse all the entreaties of her sons, that she would see the kind-hearted neighbours, who called on their way from church, to sympathize and condole. No! she would stay with the dead husband that had spoken tenderly at last, if for three years he had kept silence; who knew but what, if she had only been more gentle and less angrily reserved he might have relented earlier – and in time!

She sat rocking herself to and fro by the side of the bed, while the footsteps below went in and out; she had been in sorrow too long to have any violent burst of deep grief now; the furrows were well worn in her cheeks, and the tears flowed quietly, if incessantly, all the day long. But when the winter's night drew on, and the neighbours had gone away to their homes, she stole to the window, and gazed out, long and wistfully, over the dark grey moors. She did not hear her son's voice, as he spoke to her from the door, nor his footstep as he drew nearer. She started when he touched her.

'Mother! come down to us. There's no one but Will and me. Dearest mother, we do so want you.' The poor lad's voice trembled, and he began to cry. It appeared to require an effort on Mrs Leigh's part to tear herself away from the window, but with a sigh she complied with his request.

The two boys (for though Will was nearly twenty-one, she still thought of him as a lad) had done everything in their power to make the house-place comfortable for her. She herself, in the old days before her sorrow, had never made a brighter fire or a cleaner hearth, ready for her husband's return home, than now awaited her. The tea-things were all put out, and the kettle was boiling; and the boys had calmed their grief down into a kind of sober cheerfulness. They paid her every attention they could think of, but received little notice on her part; she did not resist – she rather submitted to all their arrangements; but they did not seem to touch her heart.

When tea was ended, – it was merely the form of tea that had been gone through, – Will moved the things away to the dresser. His mother leant back languidly in her chair.

'Mother, shall Tom read you a chapter? He's a better scholar than I.'

'Aye, lad!' said she, almost eagerly. 'That's it. Read me the Prodigal Son. Aye, aye, lad. Thank thee.'

Tom found the chapter, and read it in the high-pitched voice which is customary in village-schools. His mother bent forward, her lips parted, her eyes dilated; her whole body instinct with eager attention. Will sat with his head depressed, and hung down. He knew why that chapter had been chosen; and to him it recalled the family's disgrace. When the reading was ended, he still hung down his head in gloomy silence. But her face was brighter than it had been before for the day. Her eyes looked dreamy, as if she saw a vision; and by and by she pulled the bible towards her, and putting her finger underneath each word, began to read them aloud in a low voice to herself; she read again the words of bitter sorrow and deep humiliation; but most of all she paused and brightened over the father's tender reception of the repentant prodigal.

So passed the Christmas evening in the Upclose Farm.

The snow had fallen heavily over the dark waving moorland, before the day of the funeral. The black storm-laden dome of heaven lay very still and close upon the white earth, as they carried the body forth out of the house which had known his presence so long as its ruling power. Two and two the mourners followed, making a black procession, in their winding march over the un-beaten snow, to Milne-Row Church – now lost in some hollow of the bleak moors, now slowly climbing the heaving ascents. There was no long tarrying after the funeral, for many of the neighbours who accompanied the body to the grave had far to go, and the great white flakes which came slowly down, were the boding fore-runners of a heavy storm. One old friend alone accompanied the widow and her sons to their home.

The Upclose Farm had belonged for generations to the Leighs; and yet its possession hardly raised them above the rank of labourers. There was the house and outbuildings, all of an old-fashioned kind, and about seven acres of barren unproductive land, which they had never possessed capital enough to improve; indeed they could hardly rely upon it for subsistence; and it had been customary to bring up the sons to some trade – such as a wheelwright's, or blacksmith's.

James Leigh had left a will, in the possession of the old man who accompanied them home. He read it aloud. James had bequeathed the farm to his faithful wife, Anne Leigh, for her life-time; and afterwards, to his son William. The hundred and odd pounds in the savings'-bank was to accumulate for Thomas.

After the reading was ended, Anne Leigh sat silent for a time; and then she asked to speak to Samuel Orme alone. The sons went into the back-kitchen, and thence strolled out into the fields regardless of the driving snow. The brothers were dearly fond of each other, although they were very different in character. Will, the elder, was like his father, stern, reserved, and scrupulously upright. Tom (who was ten years younger) was gentle and delicate as a girl, both in appearance and character. He had always clung to his mother, and dreaded his father. They did not speak as they walked, for they were only in the habit of talking about facts, and hardly knew the more sophisticated language applied to the description of feelings.

Meanwhile their mother had taken hold of Samuel Orme's arm with her trembling hand.

'Samuel, I must let the farm – I must.'

'Let the farm! What's come o'er the woman?'

'Oh, Samuel!' said she, her eyes swimming in tears, 'I'm just fain to go and live in Manchester. I mun let the farm.'

Samuel looked, and pondered, but did not speak for some time. At last he said –

'If thou hast made up thy mind, there's no speaking again it; and thou must e'en go. Thou 'lt be sadly pottered wi' Manchester ways; but that's not my look out. Why, thou 'lt have to buy potatoes, a thing thou hast never done afore in all thy born life. Well! it's not my look out. It's rather for me than again me. Our Jenny is going to be married to Tom Higginbotham, and he was speaking of wanting a bit of land to begin upon. His father will be dying sometime, I reckon, and then he'll step into the Croft Farm. But meanwhile' –

'Then, thou 'lt let the farm,' said she, still as eagerly as ever.

'Aye, aye, he'll take it fast enough, I've a notion. But I'll not drive a bargain with thee just now; it would not be right; we'll wait a bit.'

'No; I cannot wait, settle it out at once.'

'Well, well; I'll speak to Will about it. I see him out yonder. I'll step to him, and talk it over.'

Accordingly he went and joined the two lads, and without more ado, began the subject to them.

'Will, thy mother is fain to go live in Manchester, and covets to let the farm. Now, I'm willing to take it for Tom Higginbotham;

but I like to drive a keen bargain, and there would be no fun chaffering with thy mother just now. Let thee and me buckle to, my lad! and try and cheat each other; it will warm us this cold day.'

'Let the farm!' said both the lads at once, with infinite surprise. 'Go live in Manchester!'

When Samuel Orme found that the plan had never before been named to either Will or Tom, he would have nothing to do with it, he said, until they had spoken to their mother; likely she was 'dazed' by her husband's death; he would wait a day or two, and not name it to any one; not to Tom Higginbotham himself, or may be he would set his heart upon it. The lads had better go in and talk it over with their mother. He bade them good day, and left them.

Will looked very gloomy, but he did not speak till they got near the house. Then he said, –

'Tom, go to th' shippon, and supper the cows. I want to speak to mother alone.'

When he entered the house-place, she was sitting before the fire, looking into its embers. She did not hear him come in; for some time she had lost her quick perception of outward things.

'Mother! what's this about going to Manchester?' asked he.

'Oh, lad!' said she, turning round, and speaking in a beseeching tone, 'I must go and seek our Lizzie. I cannot rest here for thinking on her. Many's the time I've left thy father sleeping in bed, and stole to th' window, and looked and looked my heart out towards Manchester, till I thought I must just set out and tramp over moor and moss straight away till I got there, and then lift up every downcast face till I came to our Lizzie. And often, when the south wind was blowing soft among the hollows, I've fancied (it could but be fancy, thou knowest) I heard her crying upon me; and I've thought the voice came closer and closer, till at last it was sobbing out "Mother" close to the door; and I've stolen down, and undone the latch before now, and looked out into the still black night, thinking to see her, – and turned sick and sorrowful when I heard no living sound but the sough of the wind dying away. Oh! speak not to me of stopping here, when she may be perishing for hunger, like the poor lad in the parable.' And now she lifted up her voice and wept aloud.

Will was deeply grieved. He had been old enough to be told the family shame when, more than two years before, his father had had his letter to his daughter returned by her mistress in Manchester, telling him that Lizzie had left her service some time – and why. He had sympathized with his father's stern anger; though he had thought him something hard, it is true, when he had forbidden his weeping, heart-broken wife to go and try to find her poor sinning child, and declared that henceforth they would have no daughter; that she should be as one dead, and her name never more be named at market or at meal time, in blessing or in prayer. He had held his peace, with compressed lips and contracted brow, when the neighbours had noticed to him how poor Lizzie's death had aged both his father and his mother; and how they thought the bereaved couple would never hold up their heads again. He himself had felt as if that one event had made him old before his time; and had envied Tom the tears he had shed over poor, pretty, innocent, dead Lizzie. He thought about her sometimes, till he ground his teeth together, and could have struck her down in her shame. His mother had never named her to him until now.

'Mother!' said he at last. 'She may be dead. Most likely she is.'

'No, Will; she is not dead,' said Mrs Leigh. 'God will not let her die till I've seen her once again. Thou dost not know how I've prayed and prayed just once again to see her sweet face, and tell her I've forgiven her, though she's broken my heart – she has, Will.' She could not go on for a minute or two for the choking sobs. 'Thou dost not know that, or thou wouldst not say she could be dead, – for God is very merciful, Will; He is, – He is much more pitiful than man, – I could never ha' spoken to thy father as I did to Him, – and yet thy father forgave her at last. The last words he said were that he forgave her. Thou 'lt not be harder than thy father, Will? Do not try and hinder me going to seek her, for it's no use.'

Will sat very still for a long time before he spoke. At last he said, 'I'll not hinder you. I think she's dead, but that's no matter.'

'She is not dead,' said her mother, with low earnestness. Will took no notice of the interruption.

'We will all go to Manchester for a twelve-month, and let the farm to Tom Higginbotham. I'll get blacksmith's work; and Tom can have good schooling for awhile, which he's always craving for. At the end of the year you'll come back, mother, and give over fretting for Lizzie, and think with me that she is dead, – and, to my mind, that would be more comfort than to think of her living;' he dropped his voice as he spoke these last words. She shook her head, but made no answer. He asked again, –

'Will you, mother, agree to this?'

'I'll agree to it a-this-ns,' said she. 'If I hear and see nought of her for a twelvemonth, me being in Manchester looking out, I'll just ha' broken my heart fairly before the year's ended, and then I shall know neither love nor sorrow for her any more, when I'm at rest in the grave – I'll agree to that, Will.'

'Well, I suppose it must be so. I shall not tell Tom, mother, why we're flitting to Manchester. Best spare him.'

'As thou wilt,' said she, sadly, 'so that we go, that's all.'

Before the wild daffodils were in flower in the sheltered copses round Upclose Farm, the Leighs were settled in their Manchester home; if they could ever grow to consider that place as a home, where there was no garden, or outbuilding, no fresh breezy outlet, no far-stretching view, over moor and hollow, – no dumb animals to be tended, and, what more than all they missed, no old haunting memories, even though those remembrances told of sorrow, and the dead and gone.

Mrs Leigh heeded the loss of all these things less than her sons. She had more spirit in her countenance than she had had for months, because now she had hope; of a sad enough kind, to be sure, but still it was hope. She performed all her household duties, strange and complicated as they were, and bewildered as she was with all the town-necessities of her new manner of life; but when her house was 'sided,' and the boys come home from their work, in the evening, she would put on her things and steal out, un-noticed, as she thought, but not without many a heavy sigh from Will, after she had closed the house-door and departed. It was often past midnight before she came back, pale and weary, with almost a guilty look upon her face; but that face so full of dis-appointment and hope deferred, that Will had never the heart to say what he thought of the folly and hopelessness of the search. Night after night it was renewed, till days grew to weeks and weeks to months. All this time Will did his duty towards her as well as he could, without having sympathy with her. He staid at home in the evenings for Tom's sake, and often wished he had Tom's pleasure in reading, for the time hung heavy on his hands, as he sat up for his mother.

I need not tell you how the mother spent the weary hours. And yet I will tell you something. She used to wander out, at first as if without a purpose, till she rallied her thoughts, and brought all her energies to bear on the one point; then she went with earnest patience along the least known ways to some new part of the town, looking wistfully with dumb entreaty into people's faces; sometimes catching a glimpse of a figure which had a kind of momentary likeness to her child's, and following that figure with never wearying perseverance, till some light from shop or lamp showed the cold strange face which was not her daughter's. Once or twice a kind-hearted passer-by, struck by her look of yearning woe, turned back and offered help, or asked her what she wanted. When so spoken to, she answered only, 'You don't know a poor girl they call Lizzie Leigh, do you?' and when they denied all knowledge, she shook her head, and went on again. I think they believed her to be crazy. But she never spoke first to any one. She sometimes took a few minutes' rest on the door-steps, and sometimes (very seldom) covered her face and cried; but she could not afford to lose time and chances in this way; while her eyes were blinded with tears, the lost one might pass by unseen.

One evening, in the rich time of shortening autumn-days, Will saw an old man, who, without being absolutely drunk, could not guide himself rightly along the foot-path, and was mocked for his unsteadiness of gait by the idle boys of the neighbourhood. For his father's sake Will regarded old age with tenderness, even when most degraded and removed from the stern virtues which dignified that father; so he took the old man home, and seemed to believe his often-repeated assertions that he drank nothing but water. The stranger tried to stiffen himself up into steadiness as he drew nearer home, as if there were some one there, for whose respect he cared even in his half-intoxicated state, or whose feelings he feared to grieve. His home was exquisitely clean and neat even in outside appearance; threshold, window, and window-sill, were outward signs of some spirit of purity within. Will was rewarded for his attention by a bright glance of thanks, succeeded by a blush of shame, from a young woman of twenty or thereabouts. She did not speak, or second her father's hospitable invitations to him to be seated. She seemed unwilling that a stranger should witness her father's attempts at stately sobriety, and Will could not bear to stay and see her distress. But when the old man, with many a flabby shake of the hand, kept asking him to come again some other evening and see them, Will sought her down-cast eyes, and, though he could not read their veiled meaning, he answered timidly, 'If it's agreeable to everybody, I'll come – and thank ye.' But there was no answer from the girl to whom

this speech was in reality addressed; and Will left the house liking
her all the better for never speaking.

He thought about her a great deal for the next day or two; he
scolded himself for being so foolish as to think of her, and then fell
to with fresh vigour, and thought of her more than ever. He tried
to depreciate her; he told himself she was not pretty, and then
made indignant answer that he liked her looks much better than
any beauty of them all. He wished he was not so country looking,
so red-faced, so broad-shouldered; while she was like a lady, with
her smooth colourless complexion, her bright dark hair and her
spotless dress. Pretty, or not pretty, she drew his footsteps
towards her; he could not resist the impulse that made him wish to
see her once more, and find out some fault which should unloose
his heart from her unconscious keeping. But there she was, pure
and maidenly as before. He sat and looked, answering her father at
cross-purposes, while she drew more and more into the shadow of
the chimney-corner out of sight. Then the spirit that possessed
him (it was not he himself, sure, that did so impudent a thing!)
made him get up and carry the candle to a different place, under
the pretence of giving her more light at her sewing, but, in reality,
to be able to see her better; she could not stand this much longer,
but jumped up, and said she must put her little niece to bed; and
surely, there never was, before or since, so troublesome a child of
two years old; for, though Will staid an hour and a half longer, she
never came down again. He won the father's heart, though, by his
capacity as a listener, for some people are not at all particular, and,
so that they themselves may talk on undisturbed, are not so
unreasonable as to expect attention to what they say.

Will did gather this much, however, from the old man's talk.
He had once been quite in a genteel line of business, but had failed
for more money than any greengrocer he had heard of; at least,
any who did not mix up fish and game with greengrocery proper.
This grand failure seemed to have been the event of his life, and
one on which he dwelt with a strange kind of pride. It appeared as
if at present he rested from his past exertions (in the bankrupt
line), and depended on his daughter, who kept a small school for
very young children. But all these particulars Will only remembered and understood, when he had left the house; at the time he
heard them, he was thinking of Susan. After he had made good his
footing at Mr Palmer's, he was not long, you may be sure, without
finding some reason for returning again and again. He listened to

her father, he talked to the little niece, but he looked at Susan, both while he listened and while he talked. Her father kept on insisting upon his former gentility, the details of which would have appeared very questionable to Will's mind, if the sweet, delicate, modest Susan had not thrown an inexplicable air of refinement over all she came near. She never spoke much; she was generally diligently at work; but when she moved it was so noiselessly, and when she did speak, it was in so low and soft a voice, that silence, speech, motion and stillness, alike seemed to remove her high above Will's reach into some saintly and inaccessible air of glory – high above his reach, even as she knew him! And, if she were made acquainted with the dark secret behind, of his sister's shame, which was kept ever present to his mind by his mother's nightly search among the outcast and forsaken, would not Susan shrink away from him with loathing, as if he were tainted by the involuntary relationship? This was his dread; and thereupon followed a resolution that he would withdraw from her sweet company before it was too late. So he resisted internal temptation, and staid at home, and suffered and sighed. He became angry with his mother for her untiring patience in seeking for one who, he could not help hoping, was dead rather than alive. He spoke sharply to her, and received only such sad deprecatory answers as made him reproach himself, and still more lose sight of peace of mind. This struggle could not last long without affecting his health; and Tom, his sole companion through the long evenings, noticed his increasing languor, his restless irritability, with perplexed anxiety, and at last resolved to call his mother's attention to his brother's haggard, care-worn looks. She listened with a startled recollection of Will's claims upon her love. She noticed his decreasing appetite, and half-checked sighs.

'Will, lad! what's come o'er thee?' said she to him, as he sat listlessly gazing into the fire.

'There's nought the matter with me,' said he, as if annoyed at her remark.

'Nay, lad, but there is.' He did not speak again to contradict her; indeed she did not know if he had heard her, so unmoved did he look.

'Would'st like to go back to Upclose Farm?' asked she, sorrowfully.

'It's just blackberrying time,' said Tom.

Will shook his head. She looked at him awhile, as if trying

to read that expression of despondency and trace it back to its source.

'Will and Tom could go,' said she; 'I must stay here till I've found her, thou know'st,' continued she, dropping her voice.

He turned quickly round, and with the authority he at all times exercised over Tom, bade him begone to bed.

When Tom had left the room he prepared to speak.

CHAPTER II

'Mother,' then said Will, 'why will you keep on thinking she's alive? If she were but dead, we need never name her name again. We've never heard nought on her since father wrote her that letter; we never knew whether she got it or not. She'd left her place before then. Many a one dies is – '

'Oh my lad! dunnot speak so to me, or my heart will break outright,' said his mother, with a sort of cry. Then she calmed herself, for she yearned to persuade him to her own belief. 'Thou never asked, and thou 'rt too like thy father for me to tell without asking – but it were all to be near Lizzie's old place that I settled down on this side o' Manchester; and the very day at after we came, I went to her old missus, and asked to speak a word wi' her. I had a strong mind to cast it up to her, that she should ha' sent my poor lass away without telling on it to us first; but she were in black, and looked so sad I could na' find in my heart to threep it up. But I did ask her a bit about our Lizzie. The master would have her turned away at a day's warning, (he's gone to t'other place; I hope he'll meet wi' more mercy there than he showed our Lizzie, – I do, –) and when the missus asked her should she write to us, she says Lizzie shook her head; and when she speered at her again, the poor lass went down on her knees, and begged her not, for she said it would break my heart, (as it has done, Will – God knows it has),' said the poor mother, choking with her struggle to keep down her hard overmastering grief, 'and her father would curse her – Oh, God, teach me to be patient.' She could not speak for a few minutes, – 'and the lass threatened, and said she'd go drown herself in the canal, if the missus wrote home, – and so –

'Well! I'd got a trace of my child, – the missus thought she'd gone to th' workhouse to be nursed; and there I went, – and there, sure enough, she had been, – and they'd turned her out as soon as

she were strong, and told her she were young enough to work, –
but whatten kind o'work would be open to her, lad, and her baby
to keep?'

Will listened to his mother's tale with deep sympathy, not
unmixed with the old bitter shame. But the opening of her heart
had unlocked his, and after a while he spoke.

'Mother! I think I'd e'en better go home. Tom can stay wi' thee.
I know I should stay too, but I cannot stay in peace so near – her –
without craving to see her – Susan Palmer I mean.'

'Has the old Mr Palmer thou telled me on a daughter?' asked
Mrs Leigh.

'Aye, he has. And I love her above a bit. And it's because I love
her I want to leave Manchester. That's all.'

Mrs Leigh tried to understand this speech for some time, but
found it difficult of interpretation.

'Why should'st thou not tell her thou lov'st her? Thou 'rt a
likely lad, and sure o' work. Thou 'lt have Upclose at my death;
and as for that I could let thee have it now, and keep mysel by
doing a bit of charring. It seems to me a very backwards sort o'
way of winning her to think of leaving Manchester.'

'Oh mother, she's so gentle and so good, – she's downright
holy. She's never known a touch of sin; and can I ask her to marry
me, knowing what we do about Lizzie, and fearing worse! I doubt
if one like her could ever care for me; but if she knew about my
sister, it would put a gulf between us, and she'd shudder up at the
thought of crossing it. You don't know how good she is, mother!'

'Will, Will! if she's so good as thou say'st, she'll have pity on
such as my Lizzie. If she has no pity for such, she's a cruel
Pharisee, and thou 'rt best without her.'

But he only shook his head, and sighed; and for the time the
conversation dropped.

But a new idea sprang up in Mrs Leigh's head. She thought that
she would go and see Susan Palmer, and speak up for Will, and tell
her the truth about Lizzie; and according to her pity for the poor
sinner, would she be worthy or unworthy of him. She resolved to
go the very next afternoon, but without telling any one of her
plan. Accordingly she looked out the Sunday clothes she had
never before had the heart to unpack since she came to Manchester, but which she now desired to appear in, in order to do
credit to Will. She put on her old-fashioned black mode bonnet,
trimmed with real lace; her scarlet cloth cloak, which she had had

ever since she was married; and always spotlessly clean, she set
forth on her unauthorized embassy. She knew the Palmers lived in
Crown Street, though where she had heard it she could not tell;
and modestly asking her way, she arrived in the street about a
quarter to four o'clock. She stopped to inquire the exact number,
and the woman whom she addressed told her that Susan Palmer's
school would not be loosed till four, and asked her to step in and
wait until then at her house.

'For,' said she, smiling, 'them that wants Susan Palmer wants a
kind friend of ours; so we, in a manner, call cousins. Sit down,
missus, sit down. I'll wipe the chair, so that it shanna dirty your
cloak. My mother used to wear them bright cloaks, and they're
right gradely things again a green field.'

'Han ye known Susan Palmer long?' asked Mrs Leigh, pleased
with the admiration of her cloak.

'Ever since they comed to live in our street. Our Sally goes to
her school.'

'Whatten sort of a lass is she, for I ha' never seen her?'

'Well, – as for looks, I cannot say. It's so long since I first
knowed her, that I've clean forgotten what I thought of her then.
My master says he never saw such a smile for gladdening the heart.
But may be it's not looks you're asking about. The best thing I can
say of her looks is, that she's just one a stranger would stop in the
street to ask help from if he needed it. All the little childer creeps as
close as they can to her; she'll have as many as three or four
hanging to her apron all at once.'

'Is she cocket at all?'

'Cocket, bless you! you never saw a creature less set up in all
your life. Her father's cocket enough. No! she's not cocket any
way. You've not heard much of Susan Palmer, I reckon, if you
think she's cocket. She's just one to come quietly in, and do the
very thing most wanted; little things, maybe, that any one could
do, but that few would think on, for another. She'll bring her
thimble wi' her, and mend up after the childer o' nights, – and she
writes all Betty Harker's letters to her grandchild out at service, –
and she's in nobody's way, and that's a great matter, I take it.
Here's the childer running past! School is loosed. You'll find her
now, missus, ready to hear and to help. But we none on us frab her
by going near her in school-time.'

Poor Mrs Leigh's heart began to beat, and she could almost have
turned round and gone home again. Her country breeding had

made her shy of strangers, and this Susan Palmer appeared to her like a real born lady by all accounts. So she knocked with a timid feeling at the indicated door, and when it was opened, dropped a simple curtsey without speaking. Susan had her little niece in her arms, curled up with fond endearment against her breast, but she put her gently down to the ground, and instantly placed a chair in the best corner of the room for Mrs Leigh, when she told her who she was. 'It's not Will as has asked me to come,' said the mother, apologetically, 'I'd a wish just to speak to you myself!'

Susan coloured up to her temples, and stooped to pick up the little toddling girl. In a minute or two Mrs Leigh began again.

'Will thinks you would na respect us if you knew all; but I think you could na help feeling for us in the sorrow God has put upon us; so I just put on my bonnet, and came off unknownst to the lads. Every one says you're very good, and that the Lord has keeped you from falling from his ways; but maybe you've never yet been tried and tempted as some is. I'm perhaps speaking too plain, but my heart's welly broken, and I can't be choice in my words as them who are happy can. Well now! I'll tell you the truth. Will dreads you to hear it, but I'll just tell it you. You mun know,' – but here the poor woman's words failed her, and she could do nothing but sit rocking herself backwards and forwards, with sad eyes, straight-gazing into Susan's face, as if they tried to tell the tale of agony which the quivering lips refused to utter. Those wretched stony eyes forced the tears down Susan's cheeks, and, as if this sympathy gave the mother strength, she went on in a low voice, 'I had a daughter once, my heart's darling. Her father thought I made too much on her, and that she'd grow marred staying at home; so he said she mun go among strangers, and learn to rough it. She were young, and liked the thought of seeing a bit of the world; and her father heard on a place in Manchester. Well! I'll not weary you. That poor girl were led astray; and first thing we heard on it, was when a letter of her father's was sent back by her missus, saying she'd left her place, or, to speak right, the master had turned her into the street soon as he had heard of her condition – and she not seventeen!'

She now cried aloud; and Susan wept too. The little child looked up into their faces, and, catching their sorrow, began to whimper and wail. Susan took it softly up, and hiding her face in its little neck, tried to restrain her tears, and think of comfort for the mother. At last she said:

'Where is she now?'

'Lass! I dunnot know,' said Mrs Leigh, checking her sobs to communicate this addition to her distress. 'Mrs Lomax told me she went' –

'Mrs Lomax – what Mrs Lomax?'

'Her as lives in Brabazon-street. She told me my poor wench went to the work-house fra there. I'll not speak again the dead; but if her father would but ha' letten me, – but he were one who had no notion – no, I'll not say that; best say nought. He forgave her on his death-bed. I dare say I did na go th' right way to work.'

'Will you hold the child for me one instant?' said Susan.

'Ay, if it will come to me. Childer used to be fond on me till I got the sad look on my face that scares them, I think.'

But the little girl clung to Susan; so she carried it upstairs with her. Mrs Leigh sat by herself – how long she did not know.

Susan came down with a bundle of far-worn baby-clothes.

'You must listen to me a bit, and not think too much about what I'm going to tell you. Nanny is not my niece, nor any kin to me that I know of. I used to go out working by the day. One night, as I came home, I thought some woman was following me; I turned to look. The woman, before I could see her face (for she turned it to one side), offered me something. I held out my arms by instinct: she dropped a bundle into them with a bursting sob that went straight to my heart. It was a baby. I looked round again; but the woman was gone. She had run away as quick as lightning. There was a little packet of clothes – very few – and as if they were made out of its mother's gowns, for they were large patterns to buy for a baby. I was always fond of babies; and I had not my wits about me, father says; for it was very cold, and when I'd seen as well as I could (for it was past ten) that there was no one in the street, I brought it in and warmed it. Father was very angry when he came, and said he'd take it to the workhouse the next morning, and flyted me sadly about it. But when morning came I could not bear to part with it; it had slept in my arms all night; and I've heard what workhouse bringing up is. So I told father I'd give up going out working, and stay at home and keep school, if I might only keep the baby; and after awhile, he said if I earned enough for him to have his comforts, he'd let me; but he's never taken to her. Now, don't tremble so, – I've but a little more to tell, – and maybe I'm wrong in telling it; but I used to work next door to Mrs Lomax's, in Brabazon-street, and the servants were all thick together; and I heard about Bessy (they called her) being sent away. I don't know that ever I saw her; but the time would be about fitting to this child's age, and I've sometimes fancied it was her's. And now, will you look at the little clothes that came with her – bless her!'

But Mrs Leigh had fainted. The strange joy and shame, and gushing love for the little child had overpowered her; it was some time before Susan could bring her round. There she was all trembling, sick impatience to look at the little frocks. Among them was a slip of paper which Susan had forgotten to name, that had been pinned to the bundle. On it was scrawled in a round stiff hand,

'Call her Anne. She does not cry much, and takes a deal of notice. God bless you and forgive me.'

The writing was no clue at all; the name 'Anne,' common though it was, seemed something to build upon. But Mrs Leigh recognized one of the frocks instantly, as being made out of part of a gown that she and her daughter had bought together in Rochdale.

She stood up, and stretched out her hands in the attitude of blessing over Susan's bent head.

'God bless you, and show you His mercy in your need, as you have shown it to this little child.'

She took the little creature in her arms, and smoothed away her sad looks to a smile, and kissed it fondly, saying over and over again, 'Nanny, Nanny, my little Nanny.' At last the child was soothed, and looked in her face and smiled back again.

'It has her eyes,' said she to Susan.

'I never saw her to the best of my knowledge. I think it must be her's by the frock. But where can she be?'

'God knows,' said Mrs Leigh; 'I dare not think she's dead. I'm sure she isn't.'

'No! she's not dead. Every now and then a little packet is thrust in under our door, with may be two half-crowns in it; once it was half-a-sovereign. Altogether I've got seven-and-thirty shillings wrapped up for Nanny. I never touch it, but I've often thought the poor mother feels near to God when she brings this money. Father wanted to set the policeman to watch, but I said No, for I was afraid if she was watched she might not come, and it seemed such a holy thing to be checking her in, I could not find in my heart to do it.'

'Oh, if we could but find her! I'd take her in my arms, and we'd just lie down and die together.'

'Nay, don't speak so!' said Susan gently, 'for all that's come and gone, she may turn right at last. Mary Magdalen did, you know.'

'Eh! but I were nearer right about thee than Will. He thought you would never look on him again if you knew about Lizzie. But thou 'rt not a Pharisee.'

'I'm sorry he thought I could be so hard,' said Susan in a low voice, and colouring up. Then Mrs Leigh was alarmed, and in her motherly anxiety, she began to fear lest she had injured Will in Susan's estimation.

'You see Will thinks so much of you – gold would not be good enough for you to walk on, in his eye. He said you'd never look at him as he was, let alone his being brother to my poor wench. He loves you so, it makes him think meanly on everything belonging to himself, as not fit to come near ye, – but he's a good lad, and a good son – thou 'lt be a happy woman if thou 'lt have him, – so don't let my words go against him; don't!'

But Susan hung her head and made no answer. She had not known until now, that Will thought so earnestly and seriously about her; and even now she felt afraid that Mrs Leigh's words promised her too much happiness, and that they could not be true. At any rate the instinct of modesty made her shrink from saying anything which might seem like a confession of her own feelings to a third person. Accordingly she turned the conversation on the child.

'I'm sure he could not help loving Nanny,' said she. 'There never was such a good little darling; don't you think she'd win his heart if he knew she was his niece, and perhaps bring him to think kindly on his sister?'

'I dunnot know,' said Mrs Leigh, shaking her head. 'He has a turn in his eye like his father, that makes me ——. He's right down good though. But you see I've never been a good one at managing folk; one severe look turns me sick, and then I say just the wrong thing, I'm so fluttered. Now I should like nothing better than to take Nancy home with me, but Tom knows nothing but that his sister is dead, and I've not the knack of speaking rightly to Will. I dare not do it, and that's the truth. But you mun not think badly of Will. He's so good hissel, that he can't understand how any one can do wrong; and, above all, I'm sure he loves you dearly.'

'I don't think I could part with Nancy,' said Susan, anxious to stop this revelation of Will's attachment to herself. 'He'll come round to her soon; he can't fail; and I'll keep a sharp look-out after the poor mother, and try and catch her the next time she comes with her little parcels of money.'

'Aye, lass! we mun get hold of her; my Lizzie. I love thee dearly for thy kindness to her child; but, if thou can'st catch her for me, I'll pray for thee when I'm too near my death to speak words; and while I live, I'll serve thee next to her, – she mun come first, thou know'st. God bless thee, lass. My heart is lighter by a deal than it was when I comed in. Them lads will be looking for me home, and I mun go, and leave this little sweet one,' kissing it. 'If I can take courage, I'll tell Will all that has come and gone between us two. He may come and see thee, mayn't he?'

'Father will be very glad to see him, I'm sure,' replied Susan. The way in which this was spoken satisfied Mrs Leigh's anxious heart that she had done Will no harm by what she had said; and with many a kiss to the little one, and one more fervent tearful blessing on Susan, she went homewards.

CHAPTER III

That night Mrs Leigh stopped at home; that only night for many months. Even Tom, the scholar, looked up from his books in amazement; but then he remembered that Will had not been well, and that his mother's attention having been called to the circumstance, it was only natural she should stay to watch him. And no watching could be more tender, or more complete. Her loving eyes seemed never averted from his face; his grave, sad, care-worn face. When Tom went to bed the mother left her seat, and going up to Will where he sat looking at the fire, but not seeing it, she kissed his forehead, and said,

'Will! lad, I've been to see Susan Palmer!'

She felt the start under her hand which was placed on his shoulder, but he was silent for a minute or two. Then he said,

'What took you there, mother?'

'Why, my lad, it was likely I should wish to see one you cared for; I did not put myself forward. I put on my Sunday clothes, and tried to behave as yo'd ha liked me. At least I remember trying at first; but after, I forgot all.'

She rather wished that he would question her as to what made her forget all. But he only said,

'How was she looking, mother?'

'Will, thou seest I never set eyes on her before; but she's a good gentle looking creature; and I love her dearly, as I've reason to.'

Will looked up with momentary surprise; for his mother was too shy to be usually taken with strangers. But after all it was natural in this case, for who could look at Susan without loving her? So still he did not ask any questions, and his poor mother had to take courage, and try again to introduce the subject near to her heart. But how?

'Will!' said she (jerking it out, in sudden despair of her own powers to lead to what she wanted to say), 'I told her all.'

'Mother! you've ruined me,' said he standing up, and standing opposite to her with a stern white look of affright on his face.

'No! my own dear lad; dunnot look so scared, I have not ruined you!' she exclaimed, placing her two hands on his shoulders and looking fondly into his face. 'She's not one to harden her heart against a mother's sorrow. My own lad, she's too good for that. She's not one to judge and scorn the sinner. She's too deep read in her New Testament for that. Take courage, Will; and thou mayst, for I watched her well, though it is not for one woman to let out another's secret. Sit thee down, lad, for thou look'st very white.'

He sat down. His mother drew a stool towards him, and sat at his feet.

'Did you tell her about Lizzie, then?' asked he, hoarse and low.

'I did, I told her all; and she fell a crying over my deep sorrow, and the poor wench's sin. And then a light comed into her face, trembling and quivering with some new glad thought; and what dost thou think it was, Will, lad? Nay, I'll not misdoubt but that thy heart will give thanks as mine did, afore God and His angels, for her great goodness. That little Nanny is not her niece, she's our Lizzie's own child, my little grandchild.' She could no longer restrain her tears, and they fell hot and fast, but still she looked into his face.

'Did she know it was Lizzie's child? I do not comprehend,' said he, flushing red.

'She knows now: she did not at first, but took the little helpless creature in, out of her own pitiful loving heart, guessing only that it was the child of shame and she's worked for it, and kept it, and tended it ever sin' it were a mere baby, and loves it fondly. Will! won't you love it?' asked she beseechingly.

He was silent for an instant; then he said, 'Mother, I'll try. Give me time, for all these things startle me. To think of Susan having to do with such a child!'

'Aye, Will! and to think (as may be yet) of Susan having to do with the child's mother! For she is tender and pitiful, and speaks hopefully of my lost one, and will try and find her for me, when she comes, as she does sometimes, to thrust money under the door, for her baby. Think of that, Will. Here's Susan, good and pure as the angels in heaven, yet, like them, full of hope and mercy, and one who, like them, will rejoice over her as repents. Will, my lad, I'm not afeared of you now, and I must speak, and you must listen. I am your mother, and I dare to command you, because I know I am in the right and that God is on my side. If He should lead the poor wandering lassie to Susan's door, and she comes back crying and sorrowful, led by that good angel to us once more, thou shalt never say a casting-up word to her about her sin, but be tender and helpful towards one "who was lost and is found," so may God's blessing rest on thee, and so mayst thou lead Susan home as thy wife.'

She stood, no longer as the meek, imploring, gentle mother, but firm and dignified, as if the interpreter of God's will. Her manner was so unusual and solemn, that it overcame all Will's pride and stubbornness. He rose softly while she was speaking, and bent his head as if in reverence at her words, and the solemn injunction which they conveyed. When she had spoken, he said in so subdued a voice that she was almost surprised at the sound, 'Mother, I will.'

'I may be dead and gone, – but all the same, – thou wilt take home the wandering sinner, and heal up her sorrows, and lead her to her Father's house. My lad! I can speak no more; I'm turned very faint.'

He placed her in a chair; he ran for water. She opened her eyes and smiled.

'God bless you, Will. Oh! I am so happy. It seems as if she were found; my heart is so filled with gladness.'

That night Mr Palmer stayed out late and long. Susan was afraid that he was at his old haunts and habits, – getting tipsy at some public-house; and this thought oppressed her, even though she had so much to make her happy, in the consciousness that Will loved her. She sat up long, and then she went to bed, leaving all arranged as well as she could for her father's return. She looked at the little rosy sleeping girl who was her bed-fellow, with re-doubled tenderness, and with many a prayerful thought. The little arms entwined her neck as she lay down, for Nanny was a light sleeper, and was conscious that she, who was loved with all the power of that sweet childish heart, was near her, and by her, although she was too sleepy to utter any of her half-formed words.

And by-and-bye she heard her father come home, stumbling uncertain, trying first the windows, and next the door-fastenings, with many a loud incoherent murmur. The little Innocent twined around her seemed all the sweeter and more lovely, when she thought sadly of her erring father. And presently he called aloud for a light; she had left matches and all arranged as usual on the dresser, but, fearful of some accident from fire, in his unusually intoxicated state, she now got up softly, and putting on a cloak, went down to his assistance.

Alas! the little arms that were unclosed from her soft neck belonged to a light, easily awakened sleeper. Nanny missed her darling Susy, and terrified at being left alone in the vast mysterious darkness, which had no bounds, and seemed infinite, she slipped out of bed, and tottered in her little night-gown towards the door. There was a light below, and there was Susy and safety! So she went onwards two steps towards the steep abrupt stairs; and then dazzled with sleepiness, she stood, she wavered, she fell! Down on her head on the stone floor she fell! Susan flew to her, and spoke all soft, entreating, loving words; but her white lids covered up the blue violets of eyes, and there was no murmur came out of the pale lips. The warm tears that rained down did not awaken her; she lay stiff, and weary with her short life, on Susan's knee. Susan went sick with terror. She carried her upstairs, and laid her tenderly in bed; she dressed herself most hastily, with her trembling fingers. Her father was asleep on the settle down stairs; and useless, and worse than useless if awake. But Susan flew out of the door, and down the quiet resounding street, towards the nearest doctor's house. Quickly she went; but as quickly a shadow followed, as if impelled by some sudden terror. Susan rung wildly at the night-bell, – the shadow crouched near. The doctor looked out from an upstairs window.

'A little child has fallen down stairs at No. 9, Crown-street, and is very ill, – dying I'm afraid. Please, for God's sake, sir, come directly. No. 9, Crown-street.'

'I'll be there directly,' said he, and shut the window.

'For that God you have just spoken about, – for His sake, – tell me are you Susan Palmer? Is it my child that lies a-dying?' said the shadow, springing forwards, and clutching poor Susan's arm.

'It is a little child of two years old, – I do not know whose it is; I love it as my own. Come with me, whoever you are; come with me.'

The two sped along the silent streets, – as silent as the night were they. They entered the house; Susan snatched up the light, and carried it upstairs. The other followed.

She stood with wild glaring eyes by the bedside, never looking at Susan, but hungrily gazing at the little white still child. She stooped down, and put her hand tight on her own heart, as if to still its beating, and bent her ear to the pale lips. Whatever the result was, she did not speak; but threw off the bed-clothes wherewith Susan had tenderly covered up the little creature, and felt its left side.

Then she threw up her arms with a cry of wild despair.

'She is dead! she is dead!'

She looked so fierce, so mad, so haggard, that for an instant Susan was terrified – the next, the holy God had put courage into her heart, and her pure arms were round that guilty wretched creature, and her tears were falling fast and warm upon her breast. But she was thrown off with violence.

'You killed her – you slighted her – you let her fall down those stairs! you killed her!'

Susan cleared off the thick mist before her, and gazing at the mother with her clear, sweet, angel-eyes, said mournfully –

'I would have laid down my own life for her.'

'Oh, the murder is on my soul!' exclaimed the wild bereaved mother, with the fierce impetuosity of one who has none to love her and to be beloved, regard to whom might teach self-restraint.

'Hush!' said Susan, her finger on her lips. 'Here is the doctor. God may suffer her to live.'

The poor mother turned sharp round. The doctor mounted the stair. Ah! that mother was right; the little child was really dead and gone.

And when he confirmed her judgment, the mother fell down in a fit. Susan, with her deep grief, had to forget herself, and forget her darling (her charge for years), and question the doctor what she must do with the poor wretch, who lay on the floor in such extreme of misery.

'She is the mother!' said she.

'Why did not she take better care of her child?' asked he, almost angrily.

But Susan only said, 'The little child slept with me; and it was I that left her.'

'I will go back and make up a composing draught; and while I am away you must get her to bed.'

Susan took out some of her own clothes, and softly undressed the stiff, powerless, form. There was no other bed in the house but the one in which her father slept. So she tenderly lifted the body of her darling; and was going to take it down stairs, but the mother opened her eyes, and seeing what she was about, she said,

'I am not worthy to touch her, I am so wicked; I have spoken to you as I never should have spoken; but I think you are very good; may I have my own child to lie in my arms for a little while?'

Her voice was so strange a contrast to what it had been before she had gone into the fit that Susan hardly recognized it; it was now so unspeakably soft, so irresistibly pleading, the features too had lost their fierce expression, and were almost as placid as death. Susan could not speak, but she carried the little child, and laid it in its mother's arms; then as she looked at them, something overpowered her, and she knelt down, crying aloud,

'Oh, my God, my God, have mercy on her, and forgive, and comfort her.'

But the mother kept smiling, and stroking the little face, murmuring soft tender words, as if it were alive; she was going mad, Susan thought; but she prayed on, and on, and ever still she prayed with streaming eyes.

The doctor came with the draught. The mother took it, with docile unconsciousness of its nature as medicine. The doctor sat by her; and soon she fell asleep. Then he rose softly, and beckoning Susan to the door, he spoke to her there.

'You must take the corpse out of her arms. She will not awake. That draught will make her sleep for many hours. I will call before noon again. It is now daylight. Good-bye.'

Susan shut him out; and then gently extricating the dead child from its mother's arms, she could not resist making her own quiet moan over her darling. She tried to learn off its little placid face, dumb and pale before her.

'Not all the scalding tears of care
    Shall wash away that vision fair;
  Not all the thousand thoughts that rise,
    Not all the sights that dim her eyes,
        Shall e'er usurp the place
        Of that little angel-face.'

And then she remembered what remained to be done. She saw that all was right in the house; her father was still dead asleep on the settle, in spite of all the noise of the night. She went out through the quiet streets, deserted still although it was broad daylight, and to where the Leighs lived. Mrs Leigh, who kept her country hours, was opening her window shutters. Susan took her by the arm, and, without speaking, went into the house-place. There she knelt down before the astonished Mrs Leigh, and cried as she had never done before; but the miserable night had over-powered her, and she who had gone through so much calmly, now that the pressure seemed removed could not find the power to speak.

'My poor dear! What has made thy heart so sore as to come and cry a-this-ons. Speak and tell me. Nay, cry on, poor wench, if thou canst not speak yet. It will ease the heart, and then thou canst tell me.'

'Nanny is dead!' said Susan. 'I left her to go to father, and she fell down stairs, and never breathed again. Oh, that's my sorrow! but I've more to tell. Her mother is come – is in our house! Come and see if it's your Lizzie.' Mrs Leigh could not speak, but, trembling, put on her things, and went with Susan in dizzy haste back to Crown-street.

CHAPTER IV

As they entered the house in Crown-street, they perceived that the door would not open freely on its hinges, and Susan instinct-ively looked behind to see the cause of the obstruction. She immediately recognized the appearance of a little parcel, wrapped in a scrap of newspaper, and evidently containing money. She stooped and picked it up. 'Look!' said she, sorrowfully, 'the mother was bringing this for her child last night.'

But Mrs Leigh did not answer. So near to the ascertaining if it were her lost child or no, she could not be arrested, but pressed onwards with trembling steps and a beating, fluttering heart. She entered the bed-room, dark and still. She took no heed of the little corpse, over which Susan paused, but she went straight to the bed, and withdrawing the curtain, saw Lizzie, – but not the former Lizzie, bright, gay, buoyant, and undimmed. This Lizzie was old before her time; her beauty was gone; deep lines of care, and alas! of want (or thus the mother imagined) were printed on the cheek, so round, and fair, and smooth, when last she gladdened her mother's eyes. Even in her sleep she bore the look of woe and despair which was the prevalent expression of her face by day; even in her sleep she had forgotten how to smile. But all these marks of the sin and sorrow she had passed through only made her mother love her the more. She stood looking at her with greedy eyes, which seemed as though no gazing could satisfy their longing; and at last she stooped down and kissed the pale, worn hand that lay outside the bed-clothes. No touch disturbed the sleeper; the mother need not have laid the hand so gently down upon the counter-pane. There was no sign of life, save only now and then a deep sob-like sigh. Mrs Leigh sat down beside the bed, and, still holding back the curtain, looked on and on, as if she could never be satisfied.

Susan would fain have stayed by her darling one; but she had many calls upon her time and thoughts, and her will had now, as ever, to be given up to that of others. All seemed to devolve the burden of their cares on her. Her father, ill-humoured from his last night's intemperance, did not scruple to reproach her with being the cause of little Nanny's death; and when, after bearing his upbraiding meekly for some time, she could no longer restrain herself, but began to cry, he wounded her even more by his injudicious attempts at comfort: for he said it was as well the child was dead; it was none of theirs, and why should they be troubled with it? Susan wrung her hands at this, and came and stood before her father, and implored him to forbear. Then she had to take all requisite steps for the coroner's inquest; she had to arrange for the dismissal of her school; she had to summon a little neighbour, and send his willing feet on a message to William Leigh, who, she felt, ought to be informed of his mother's whereabouts, and of the whole state of affairs. She asked her messenger to tell him to come and speak to her, – that his mother was at her house. She was thankful that her father sauntered out to have a gossip at the nearest coach-stand, and to relate as many of the night's adventures as he knew; for as yet he was in ignorance of the watcher and the watched, who silently passed away the hours upstairs.

At dinner-time Will came. He looked red, glad, impatient, excited. Susan stood calm and white before him, her soft, loving eyes gazing straight into his.

'Will,' said she, in a low, quiet voice, 'your sister is upstairs.'

'My sister!' said he, as if affrighted at the idea, and losing his glad look in one of gloom. Susan saw it, and her heart sank a little, but she went on as calm to all appearance as ever.

'She was little Nanny's mother, as perhaps you know. Poor little Nanny was killed last night by a fall down stairs.' All the calmness was gone; all the suppressed feeling was displayed in spite of every effort. She sat down, and hid her face from him, and cried bitterly. He forgot everything but the wish, the longing to comfort her. He put his arm round her waist, and bent over her. But all he could say, was, 'Oh, Susan, how can I comfort you! Don't take on so, – pray don't!' He never changed the words, but the tone varied every time he spoke. At last she seemed to regain her power over herself; and she wiped her eyes, and once more looked upon him with her own quiet, earnest, unfearing gaze.

'Your sister was near the house. She came in on hearing my words to the doctor. She is asleep now, and your mother is watching her. I wanted to tell you all myself. Would you like to see your mother?'

'No!' said he. 'I would rather see none but thee. Mother told me thou knew'st all.' His eyes were downcast in their shame.

But the holy and pure, did not lower or veil her eyes.

She said, 'Yes, I know all – all but her sufferings. Think what they must have been!'

He made answer low and stern, 'She deserved them all; every jot.'

'In the eye of God, perhaps she does. He is the judge: we are not.'

'Oh!' she said with a sudden burst, 'Will Leigh! I have thought so well of you; don't go and make me think you cruel and hard. Goodness is not goodness unless there is mercy and tenderness with it. There is your mother who has been nearly heart-broken, now full of rejoicing over her child – think of your mother.'

'I do think of her,' said he. 'I remember the promise I gave her

last night. Thou shouldst give me time. I would do right in time. I
never think it o'er in quiet. But I will do what is right and fitting,
never fear. Thou hast spoken out very plain to me; and mis-
doubted me, Susan; I love thee so, that thy words cut me. If I did
hang back a bit from making sudden promises, it was because not
even for love of thee, would I say what I was not feeling; and at
first I could not feel all at once as thou wouldst have me. But I'm
not cruel and hard; for if I had been, I should na' have grieved as I
have done.'

He made as if he were going away; and indeed he did feel he
would rather think it over in quiet. But Susan, grieved at her
incautious words, which had all the appearance of harshness, went
a step or two nearer – paused – and then, all over blushes, said in a
low soft whisper –

'Oh Will! I beg your pardon. I am very sorry – won't you
forgive me?'

She who had always drawn back, and been so reserved, said this
in the very softest manner; with eyes now uplifted beseechingly,
now dropped to the ground. Her sweet confusion told more than
words could do; and Will turned back, all joyous in his certainty
of being beloved, and took her in his arms and kissed her.

'My own Susan!' he said.

Meanwhile the mother watched her child in the room above.

It was late in the afternoon before she awoke; for the sleeping
draught had been very powerful. The instant she awoke, her eyes
were fixed on her mother's face with a gaze as unflinching as if
she were fascinated. Mrs Leigh did not turn away; nor move. For
it seemed as if motion would unlock the stony command
over herself which, while so perfectly still, she was enabled to
preserve. But by-and-bye Lizzie cried out in a piercing voice of
agony –

'Mother, don't look at me! I have been so wicked!' and instantly
she hid her face, and grovelled among the bedclothes, and lay like
one dead – so motionless was she.

Mrs Leigh knelt down by the bed, and spoke in the most
soothing tones.

'Lizzie, dear, don't speak so. I'm thy mother, darling; don't be
afeard of me. I never left off loving thee, Lizzie. I was always
a-thinking of thee. Thy father forgave thee afore he died.' (There
was a little start here, but no sound was heard.) 'Lizzie, lass, I'll do
aught for thee; I'll live for thee; only don't be afeard of me.

Whate'er thou art or hast been, we'll ne'er speak on 't. We'll leave th' oud times behind us, and go back to the Upclose Farm. I but left it to find thee, my lass; and God has led me to thee. Blessed be His name. And God is good too, Lizzie. Thou hast not forgot thy Bible, I'll be bound, for thou wert always a scholar. I'm no reader, but I learnt off them texts to comfort me a bit, and I've said them many a time a day to myself. Lizzie, lass, don't hide thy head so, it's thy mother as is speaking to thee. Thy little child clung to me only yesterday; and if it's gone to be an angel, it will speak to God for thee. Nay, don't sob a that 'as; thou shalt have it again in Heaven; I know thou 'lt strive to get there, for thy little Nanny's sake – and listen! I'll tell thee God's promises to them that are penitent – only doan't be afeard.'

Mrs Leigh folded her hands, and strove to speak very clearly, while she repeated every tender and merciful text she could remember. She could tell from the breathing that her daughter was listening; but she was so dizzy and sick herself when she had ended, that she could not go on speaking. It was all she could do to keep from crying aloud.

At last she heard her daughter's voice.

'Where have they taken her to?' she asked.

'She is down stairs. So quiet, and peaceful, and happy she looks.'

'Could she speak? Oh, if God – if I might but have heard her little voice! Mother, I used to dream of it. May I see her once again – Oh mother, if I strive very hard, and God is very merciful, and I go to heaven, I shall not know her – I shall not know my own again – she will shun me as a stranger and cling to Susan Palmer and to you. Oh woe! Oh woe!' She shook with exceeding sorrow.

In her earnestness of speech she had uncovered her face, and tried to read Mrs Leigh's thoughts through her looks. And when she saw those aged eyes brimming full of tears, and marked the quivering lips, she threw her arms round the faithful mother's neck, and wept there as she had done in many a childish sorrow; but with a deeper, a more wretched grief.

Her mother hushed her on her breast; and lulled her as if she were a baby; and she grew still and quiet.

They sat thus for a long, long time. At last Susan Palmer came up with some tea and bread and butter for Mrs Leigh. She watched the mother feed her sick, unwilling child, with every fond inducement to eat which she could devise; they neither of them took notice of Susan's presence. That night they lay in each other's arms; but Susan slept on the ground beside them.

They took the little corpse (the little unconscious sacrifice, whose early calling-home had reclaimed her poor wandering mother), to the hills, which in her life-time she had never seen. They dared not lay her by the stern grand-father in Milne-Row churchyard, but they bore her to a lone moorland graveyard, where long ago the quakers used to bury their dead. They laid her there on the sunny slope, where the earliest spring-flowers blow.

Will and Susan live at the Upclose Farm. Mrs Leigh and Lizzie dwell in a cottage so secluded that, until you drop into the very hollow where it is placed, you do not see it. Tom is a schoolmaster in Rochdale, and he and Will help to support their mother. I only know that, if the cottage be hidden in a green hollow of the hills, every sound of sorrow in the whole upland is heard there – every call of suffering or of sickness for help is listened to, by a sad, gentle-looking woman, who rarely smiles (and when she does, her smile is more sad than other people's tears), but who comes out of her seclusion whenever there's a shadow in any household. Many hearts bless Lizzie Leigh, but she – she prays always and ever for forgiveness – such forgiveness as may enable her to see her child once more. Mrs Leigh is quiet and happy. Lizzie is to her eyes something precious, – as the lost piece of silver – found once more. Susan is the bright one who brings sunshine to all. Children grow around her and call her blessed. One is called Nanny. Her, Lizzy often takes to the sunny graveyard in the uplands, and while the little creature gathers the daisies, and makes chains, Lizzie sits by a little grave, and weeps bitterly.

THE WELL OF PEN-MORFA

CHAPTER I

Of a hundred travellers who spend a night at Trê-Madoc, in North
Wales, there is not one, perhaps, who goes to the neighbouring
village of Pen-Morfa. The new town, built by Mr Maddocks,
Shelley's friend, has taken away all the importance of the ancient
village – formerly, as its name imports, 'the head of the marsh;'
that marsh which Mr Maddocks drained and dyked, and reclaimed from the Traeth Mawr, till Pen-Morfa, against the walls
of whose cottages the winter tides lashed in former days, has come
to stand high and dry, three miles from the sea, on a disused road
to Caernarvon. I do not think there has been a new cottage built in
Pen-Morfa this hundred years; and many an old one has dates in
some obscure corner which tell of the fifteenth century. The joists
of timber, where they meet overhead, are blackened with the
smoke of centuries. There is one large room, round which the
beds are built like cupboards, with wooden doors to open and
shut; somewhat in the old Scotch fashion, I imagine; and below
the bed (at least in one instance I can testify that this was the case,
and I was told it was not uncommon), is a great wide wooden
drawer, which contained the oat-cake, baked for some months'
consumption by the family. They call the promontory of Llyn
(the point at the end of Caernarvonshire), *Welsh* Wales: I think
they might call Pen-Morfa a Welsh Welsh village; it is so national
in its ways, and buildings, and inhabitants, and so different from
the towns and hamlets into which the English throng in summer.
How these said inhabitants of Pen-Morfa ever are distinguished
by their names, I, uninitiated, cannot tell. I only know for a fact,
that in a family there with which I am acquainted, the eldest son's
name is John Jones, because his father's was John Thomas; that
the second son is called David Williams, because his grandfather
was William Wynn, and that the girls are called indiscriminately
by the names of Thomas and Jones. I have heard some of the

Welsh chuckle over the way in which they have baffled the barristers at Caernarvon Assizes, denying the name under which they had been subpœnaed to give evidence, if they were unwilling witnesses. I could tell you of a great deal which is peculiar and wild in these true Welsh people, who are what I suppose we English were a century ago; but I must hasten on to my tale.

I have received great, true, beautiful kindness, from one of the members of the family of whom I just now spoke as living at Pen-Morfa; and when I found that they wished me to drink tea with them, I gladly did so, though my friend was the only one in the house who could speak English at all fluently. After tea, I went with them to see some of their friends; and it was then I saw the interiors of the houses of which I have spoken. It was an autumn evening; we left mellow sunset-light in the open air when we entered the houses, in which all seemed dark, save in the ruddy sphere of the firelight, for the windows were very small, and deep-set in the thick walls. Here were an old couple, who welcomed me in Welsh; and brought forth milk and oat-cake with patriarchal hospitality. Sons and daughters had married away from them; they lived alone; he was blind, or nearly so; and they sat one on each side of the fire, so old and so still (till we went in and broke the silence) that they seemed to be listening for death. At another house lived a woman stern and severe-looking. She was busy hiving a swarm of bees, alone and unassisted. I do not think my companion would have chosen to speak to her, but seeing her out in her hill-side garden, she made some inquiry in Welsh, which was answered in the most mournful tone I ever heard in my life; a voice of which the freshness and 'timbre' had been choked up by tears long years ago. I asked who she was. I dare say the story is common enough, but the sight of the woman, and her few words had impressed me. She had been the beauty of Pen-Morfa; had been in service; had been taken to London by the family whom she served; had come down, in a year or so, back to Pen-Morfa, her beauty gone into that sad, wild, despairing look, which I saw; and she about to become a mother. Her father had died during her absence, and left her a very little money; and after her child was born she took the little cottage where I saw her, and made a scanty living by the produce of her bees. She associated with no one. One event had made her savage and distrustful to her kind. She kept so much aloof that it was some time before it became known that her child was deformed, and had lost the use of its lower limbs. Poor thing! When I saw the mother, it had been for fifteen years bed-ridden. But go past when you would, in the night, you saw a light burning; it was often that of the watching mother, solitary and friendless, soothing the moaning child; or you might hear her crooning some old Welsh air, in hopes to still the pain with the loud monotonous music. Her sorrow was so dignified, and her mute endurance and her patient love won her such respect, that the neighbours would fain have been friends; but she kept alone and solitary. This a most true story. I hope that woman and her child are dead now, and their souls above.

Another story which I heard of these old primitive dwellings I mean to tell at somewhat greater length: –

There are rocks high above Pen-Morfa; they are the same that hang over Trê-Madoc, but near Pen-Morfa they sweep away, and are lost in the plain. Everywhere they are beautiful. The great sharp ledges, which would otherwise look hard and cold, are adorned with the brightest-coloured moss, and the golden lichen. Close to, you see the scarlet leaves of the crane's-bill, and the tufts of purple heather, which fill up every cleft and cranny; but in the distance you see only the general effect of infinite richness of colour, broken here and there by great masses of ivy. At the foot of these rocks come a rich verdant meadow or two; and then you are at Pen-Morfa. The village well is sharp down under the rocks. There are one or two large sloping pieces of stone in that last field, on the road leading to the well, which are always slippery; slippery in the summer's heat, almost as much as in the frost of winter, when some little glassy stream that runs over them is turned into a thin sheet of ice. Many, many years back – a lifetime ago – there lived in Pen-Morfa a widow and her daughter. Very little is required in those out-of-the-way Welsh villages. The wants of the people are very simple. Shelter, fire, a little oat-cake and buttermilk, and garden produce; perhaps some pork and bacon from the pig in winter; clothing, which is principally of home manufacture, and of the most enduring kind: these take very little money to purchase, especially in a district into which the large capitalists have not yet come, to buy up two or three acres of the peasants; and nearly every man about Pen-Morfa owned, at the time of which I speak, his dwelling and some land beside.

Eleanor Gwynn inherited the cottage (by the road-side, on the left-hand as you go from Trê-Madoc to Pen-Morfa), in which she and her husband had lived all their married life, and a small garden sloping southwards, in which her bees lingered before winging their way to the more distant heather. She took rank among her neighbours as the possessor of a moderate independence – not rich, and not poor. But the young men of Pen-Morfa thought her very rich in the possession of a most lovely daughter. Most of us know how very pretty Welsh women are; but from all accounts, Nest Gwynn (Nest, or Nesta, is the Welsh for Agnes) was more regularly beautiful than any one for miles around. The Welsh are still fond of triads, and 'as beautiful as a summer's morning at sun-rise, as a white sea-gull on the green sea-wave, and as Nest Gwynn,' is yet a saying in that district. Nest knew she was beautiful, and delighted in it. Her mother sometimes checked her in her happy pride, and sometimes reminded her that beauty was a great gift of God (for the Welsh are a very pious people); but when she began her little homily, Nest came dancing to her, and knelt down before her, and put her face up to be kissed, and so with a sweet interruption she stopped her mother's lips. Her high spirits made some few shake their heads, and some called her a flirt and a coquette; for she could not help trying to please all, both old and young, both men and women. A very little from Nest sufficed for this; a sweet glittering smile, a word of kindness, a merry glance, or a little sympathy, all these pleased and attracted; she was like the fairy-gifted child, and dropped inestimable gifts. But some who had interpreted her smiles and kind words rather as their wishes led them than as they were really warranted, found that the beautiful, beaming Nest could be decided and saucy enough, and so they revenged themselves by calling her a flirt. Her mother heard it and sighed; but Nest only laughed.

It was her work to fetch water for the day's use from the well I told you about. Old people say it was the prettiest sight in the world to see her come stepping lightly and gingerly over the stones with the pail of water balanced on her head; she was too adroit to need to steady it with her hand. They say, now that they can afford to be charitable and speak the truth, that in all her changes to other people, there never was a better daughter to a widowed mother than Nest. There is a picturesque old farmhouse under Moel Gwynn, on the road from Trê-Madoc to Criccaeth, called by some Welsh name which I now forget; but its meaning in English is 'The End of Time;' a strange, boding, ominous name. Perhaps the builder meant his work to endure till the end of time. I do not know; but there the old house stands, and will stand for many a year. When Nest was young, it belonged to one Edward Williams; his mother was dead, and people said he was on the look-out for a wife. They told Nest so, but she tossed her head and reddened, and said she thought he might look long before he got one; so it was not strange that one morning when she went to the well, one autumn morning when the dew lay heavy on the grass, and the thrushes were busy among the mountain-ash berries, Edward Williams happened to be there, on his way to the coursing match near, and somehow his greyhounds threw her pail of water over in their romping play, and she was very long in filling it again; and when she came home she threw her arms round her mother's neck, and in a passion of joyous tears told her that Edward Williams of The End of Time had asked her to marry him, and that she had said 'Yes.'

Eleanor Gwynn shed her tears too; but they fell quietly when she was alone. She was thankful Nest had found a protector – one suitable in age and apparent character, and above her in fortune; but she knew she should miss her sweet daughter in a thousand household ways; miss her in the evenings by the fireside; miss her when at night she wakened up with a start from a dream of her youth, and saw her fair face lying calm in the moonlight, pillowed by her side. Then she forgot her dream, and blessed her child, and slept again. But who could be so selfish as to be sad when Nest was so supremely happy? She danced and sang more than ever; and then sat silent, and smiled to herself: if spoken to, she started and came back to the present with a scarlet blush, which told what she had been thinking of.

That was a sunny, happy, enchanted autumn. But the winter was nigh at hand; and with it came sorrow. One fine frosty morning, Nest went out with her lover – she to the well, he to some farming business, which was to be transacted at the little inn of Pen-Morfa. He was late for his appointment; so he left her at the entrance of the village, and hastened to the inn; and she, in her best cloak and new hat (put on against her mother's advice; but they were a recent purchase, and very becoming), went through the Dol Mawr, radiant with love and happiness. One who lived until lately, met her going down towards the well, that morning; and said he turned round to look after her, she seemed unusually lovely. He wondered at the time at her wearing her Sunday clothes; for the pretty, hooded blue-cloth cloak is kept among the Welsh women as a church and market garment, and not commonly used even on the coldest days of winter for such household errands as fetching water from the well. However, as he said, 'It was not possible to look in her face, and "fault" anything she wore.' Down the sloping stones the girl went blithely with her pail. She filled it at the well: and then she took off her hat, tied the strings together, and slung it over her arm; she lifted the heavy pail and balanced it on her head. But alas! in going up the smooth, slippery, treacherous rock, the encumbrance of her cloak – it might be such a trifle as her slung hat – something, at any rate, took away her evenness of poise; the freshet had frozen on the slanting stone, and was one coat of ice; poor Nest fell, and put out her hip. No more flushing rosy colour on that sweet face – no more look of beaming innocent happiness; – instead, there was deadly pallor, and filmy eyes, over which dark shades seemed to chase each other as the shoots of agony grew more and more intense. She screamed once or twice; but the exertion (involuntary, and forced out of her by excessive pain) overcame her, and she fainted. A child coming an hour or so afterwards on the same errand, saw her lying there, ice-glued to the stone, and thought she was dead. It flew crying back.

'Nest Gwynn is dead! Nest Gwynn is dead!' and, crazy with fear, it did not stop until it had hid its head in its mother's lap. The village was alarmed, and all who were able went in haste towards the well. Poor Nest had often thought she was dying in that dreary hour; had taken fainting for death, and struggled against it; and prayed that God would keep her alive till she could see her lover's face once more; and when she did see it, white with terror, bending over her, she gave a feeble smile, and let herself faint away into unconsciousness.

Many a month she lay on her bed unable to move. Sometimes she was delirious, sometimes worn-out into the deepest depression. Through all, her mother watched her with tenderest care. The neighbours would come and offer help. They would bring presents of country dainties; and I do not suppose that there was a better dinner than ordinary cooked in any household in Pen-Morfa parish, but a portion of it was sent to Eleanor Gwynn, if not for her sick daughter, to try and tempt her herself to eat and be strengthened; for to no one would she delegate the duty of watching over her child. Edward Williams was for a long time most assiduous in his inquiries and attentions; but by-and-by (ah! you see the dark fate of poor Nest now), he slackened, so little at first that Eleanor blamed herself for her jealousy on her daughter's behalf, and chid her suspicious heart. But as spring ripened into summer, and Nest was still bedridden, Edward's coolness was visible to more than the poor mother. The neighbours would have spoken to her about it, but she shrunk from the subject as if they were probing a wound. 'At any rate,' thought she, 'Nest shall be strong before she is told about it. I will tell lies – I shall be forgiven – but I must save my child; and when she is stronger, perhaps I may be able to comfort her. Oh! I wish she would not speak to him so tenderly and trustfully, when she is delirious. I could curse him when she does.' And then Nest would call for her mother, and Eleanor would go, and invent some strange story about the summonses Edward had had to Caernarvon assizes, or to Harlech cattle market. But at last she was driven to her wits' end; it was three weeks since he had even stopped at the door to inquire, and Eleanor, mad with anxiety about her child, who was silently pining off to death for want of tidings of her lover, put on her cloak, when she had lulled her daughter to sleep one fine June evening, and set off to 'The End of Time.' The great plain which stretches out like an amphitheatre, in the half-circle of hills formed by the ranges of Moel Gwynn and the Trê-Madoc Rocks, was all golden-green in the mellow light of sunset. To Eleanor it might have been black with winter frost, she never noticed outward things till she reached The End of Time; and there, in the little farm-yard, she was brought to a sense of her present hour and errand by seeing Edward. He was examining some hay, newly stacked; the air was scented by its fragrance, and by the lingering sweetness of the breath of the cows. When Edward turned round at the footstep and saw Eleanor, he coloured and looked confused; however, he came forward to meet her in a cordial manner enough.

'It's a fine evening,' said he. 'How is Nest? But, indeed, you're being here is a sign she is better. Won't you come in and sit down?' He spoke hurriedly, as if affecting a welcome which he did not feel.

'Thank you. I'll just take this milking-stool and sit down here. The open air is like balm after being shut up so long.'

'It is a long time,' he replied, 'more than five months.'

Mrs Gwynn was trembling at heart. She felt an anger which she did not wish to show; for, if by any manifestations of temper or resentment she lessened or broke the waning thread of attachment which bound him to her daughter, she felt she should never forgive herself. She kept inwardly saying, 'Patience, patience! he may be true and love her yet;' but her indignant convictions gave her words the lie.

'It's a long time, Edward Williams, since you've been near us to ask after Nest;' said she. 'She may be better, or she may be worse, for aught you know.' She looked up at him reproachfully, but spoke in a gentle quiet tone.

'I – you see the hay has been a long piece of work. The weather has been fractious – and a master's eye is needed. Besides,' said he, as if he had found the reason for which he sought to account for his absence, 'I have heard of her from Rowland Jones. I was at the surgery for some horse-medicine – he told me about her:' and a shade came over his face, as he remembered what the doctor had said. Did he think that shade would escape the mother's eye?

'You saw Rowland Jones! Oh, man-alive, tell me what he said of my girl! He'll say nothing to me, but just hems and haws the more I pray him. But you will tell me. You *must* tell me.' She stood up and spoke in a tone of command, which his feeling of independence, weakened just then by an accusing conscience, did not enable him to resist. He strove to evade the question, however.

'It was an unlucky day that ever she went to the well!'

'Tell me what the doctor said of my child,' repeated Mrs Gwynn. 'Will she live, or will she die?' He did not dare to disobey the imperious tone in which this question was put.

'Oh, she will live, don't be afraid. The doctor said she would live.' He did not mean to lay any peculiar emphasis on the word 'live,' but somehow he did, and she, whose every nerve vibrated with anxiety, caught the word.

'She will live!' repeated she. 'But there is something behind. Tell me, for I will know. If you won't say, I'll go to Rowland Jones to-night and make him tell me what he has said to you.'

There had passed something in this conversation between himself and the doctor, which Edward did not wish to have known; and Mrs Gwynn's threat had the desired effect. But he looked vexed and irritated.

'You have such impatient ways with you, Mrs Gwynn,' he remonstrated.

'I am a mother asking news of my sick child,' said she. 'Go on. What did he say? She'll live – ' as if giving the clue.

'She'll live, he has no doubt of that. But he thinks – now don't clench your hands so – I can't tell you if you look in that way; you are enough to frighten a man.'

'I'm not speaking,' said she in a low husky tone. 'Never mind my looks: she'll live – '

'But she'll be a cripple for life. – There! you would have it out,' said he, sulkily.

'A cripple for life,' repeated she, slowly. 'And I'm one-and-twenty years older than she is!' She sighed heavily.

'And, as we're about it, I'll just tell you what is in my mind,' said he, hurried and confused. 'I've a deal of cattle; and the farm makes heavy work, as much as an able healthy woman can do. So you see – ' He stopped, wishing her to understand his meaning without words. But she would not. She fixed her dark eyes on him, as if reading his soul, till he flinched under her gaze.

'Well,' said she, at length, 'say on. Remember I've a deal of work in me yet, and what strength is mine is my daughter's.'

'You're very good. But, altogether, you must be aware, Nest will never be the same as she was.'

'And you've not yet sworn in the face of God to take her for better, for worse; and, as she is worse' – she looked in his face, caught her breath, and went on – 'as she is worse, why, you cast her off, not being church-tied to her. Though her body may be crippled, her poor heart is the same – alas! – and full of love for you. Edward, you don't mean to break it off because of our sorrows. You're only trying me, I know,' said she, as if begging him to assure her that her fears were false. 'But, you see, I'm a foolish woman – a poor foolish woman – and ready to take fright at a few words.' She smiled up in his face; but it was a forced doubting smile, and his face still retained its sullen dogged aspect.

'Nay, Mrs Gwynn,' said he, 'you spoke truth at first. Your own good sense told you Nest would never be fit to be any man's wife – unless indeed, she could catch Mr Griffiths of Tynwntyrybwlch; he might keep her a carriage, may-be.' Edward really did not mean to be unfeeling; but he was obtuse, and wished to carry off his embarrassment by a kind of friendly joke, which he had no idea would sting the poor mother as it did. He was startled at her manner.

'Put it in words like a man. Whatever you mean by my child, say it for yourself, and don't speak as if my good sense had told me any thing. I stand here, doubting my own thoughts, cursing my own fears. Don't be a coward. I ask you whether you, and Nest are troth-plight?'

'I am not a coward. Since you ask me, I answer, Nest, and I *were* troth-plight; but we *are* not. I cannot – no one would expect me to wed a cripple. It's your own doing I've told you now; I had made up my mind, but I should have waited a bit before telling you.'

'Very well,' said she, and she turned to go away; but her wrath burst the flood-gates, and swept away discretion and forethought. She moved, and stood in the gateway. Her lips parted, but no sound came; with an hysterical motion she threw her arms suddenly up to heaven, as if bringing down lightning towards the grey old house to which she pointed as they fell, and then she spoke: –

'The widow's child is unfriended. As surely as the Saviour brought the son of a widow from death to life, for her tears and cries, so surely will God and His angels watch over my Nest, and avenge her cruel wrongs.' She turned away weeping, and wringing her hands.

Edward went in-doors: he had no more desire to reckon his stores; he sat by the fire, looking gloomily at the red ashes. He might have been there half-an-hour or more, when some one knocked at the door. He would not speak. He wanted no one's company. Another knock sharp and loud. He did not speak. Then the visitor opened the door; and, to his surprise – almost to his affright – Eleanor Gwynn came in.

'I knew you were here. I knew you could not go out into the clear holy night, as if nothing had happened. Oh! did I curse you? If I did, I beg you to forgive me; and I will try and ask the Almighty to bless you, if you will but have a little mercy – a very little. It will kill my Nest if she knows the truth now – she is so very weak. Why, she cannot feed herself, she is so low and feeble. You would not wish to kill her, I think, Edward!' She looked at him as if expecting an answer; but he did not speak. She went down on her knees on the flags by him.

'You will give me a little time, Edward, to get her strong, won't you, now? I ask it on my bended knees! Perhaps, if I promise never to curse you again, you will come sometimes to see her, till she is well enough to know how all is over, and her heart's hopes crushed. Only say you'll come for a month, or so, as if you still loved her – the poor cripple – forlorn of the world. I'll get her strong, and not tax you long.' Her tears fell too fast for her to go on.

'Get up, Mrs Gwynn,' Edward said. 'Don't kneel to me. I have no objection to come and see Nest, now and then, so that all is clear between you and me. Poor thing! I'm sorry, as it happens, she's so taken up with the thought of me.'

'It was likely, was not it? and you to have been her husband before this time, if – Oh, miserable me! to let my child go and dim her bright life! But you'll forgive me, and come sometimes, just for a little quarter of an hour, once or twice a-week. Perhaps she'll be asleep sometimes when you call, and then, you know, you need not come in. If she were not so ill, I'd never ask you.'

So low and humble was the poor widow brought, through her exceeding love for her daughter.

CHAPTER II

Nest revived during the warm summer weather. Edward came to see her, and stayed the allotted quarter of an hour; but he dared not look her in the face. She was indeed a cripple: one leg was much shorter than the other, and she halted on a crutch. Her face, formerly so brilliant in colour, was wan and pale with suffering: the bright roses were gone, never to return. Her large eyes were sunk deep down in their hollow, cavernous sockets; but the light was in them still, when Edward came. Her mother dreaded her returning strength – dreaded, yet desired it; for the heavy burden of her secret was most oppressive at times, and she thought Edward was beginning to weary of his enforced attentions. One October evening she told her the truth. She even compelled her rebellious heart to take the cold, reasoning side of the question; and she told her child that her disabled frame was a disqualification for ever becoming a farmer's wife. She spoke hardly, because her inner agony and sympathy was such, she dared not trust herself to express the feelings that were rending her. But Nest turned away from cold reason; she revolted from her mother; she revolted from the world. She bound her sorrow tight up in her breast, to corrode and fester there.

Night after night, her mother heard her cries and moans – more pitiful, by far, than those wrung from her by bodily pain a year before; and night after night, if her mother spoke to soothe, she proudly denied the existence of any pain but what was physical, and consequent upon her accident.

'If she would but open her sore heart to me – to me, her mother,' Eleanor wailed forth in prayer to God, 'I would be content. Once it was enough to have my Nest all my own. Then came love, and I knew it would never be as before; and then I thought the grief I felt, when Edward spoke to me, was as sharp a sorrow as could be; but this present grief, Oh Lord, my God, is worst of all; and Thou only, Thou, canst help!'

When Nest grew as strong as she was ever likely to be on earth, she was anxious to have as much labour as she could bear. She would not allow her mother to spare her anything. Hard work – bodily fatigue – she seemed to crave. She was glad when she was stunned by exhaustion into a dull insensibility of feeling. She was almost fierce when her mother, in those first months of convalescence, performed the household tasks which had formerly been hers; but she shrank from going out of doors. Her mother thought that she was unwilling to expose her changed appearance to the neighbours' remarks; but Nest was not afraid of that: she was afraid of their pity, as being one deserted and cast off. If Eleanor gave way before her daughter's imperiousness, and sat by while Nest 'tore' about her work with the vehemence of a bitter heart, Eleanor could have cried, but she durst not; tears, or any mark of commiseration, irritated the crippled girl so much, she even drew away from caresses. Everything was to go on as it had been before she had known Edward; and so it did, outwardly; but they trod carefully, as if the ground on which they moved was hollow – deceptive. There was no more careless ease; every word was guarded, and every action planned. It was a dreary life to both. Once, Eleanor brought in a little baby, a neighbour's child, to try and tempt Nest out of herself, by her old love of children. Nest's pale face flushed as she saw the innocent child in her mother's arms; and, for a moment, she made as if she would have taken it; but then, she turned away, and hid her face behind her apron, and murmured, 'I shall never have a child to lie in my breast, and call me mother!' In a minute she arose, with compressed and tightened lips, and went about her household work, without her noticing the cooing baby again, till Mrs Gwynn, heart-sick at the failure of her little plan, took it back to its parents.

One day the news ran through Pen-Morfa that Edward Williams was about to be married. Eleanor had long expected this intelligence. It came upon her like no new thing; but it was the filling-up of her cup of woe. She could not tell Nest. She sat listlessly in the house, and dreaded that each neighbour who came in would speak about the village news. At last some one did. Nest looked round from her employment, and talked of the event with a kind of cheerful curiosity as to the particulars, which made her informant go away, and tell others that Nest had quite left off caring for Edward Williams. But when the door was shut, and Eleanor and she were left alone, Nest came and stood before her weeping mother like a stern accuser.

'Mother, why did not you let me die? Why did you keep me alive for this?' Eleanor could not speak, but she put her arms out towards her girl. Nest turned away, and Eleanor cried aloud in her soreness of spirit. Nest came again.

'Mother, I was wrong. You did your best. I don't know how it is I am so hard and cold. I wish I had died when I was a girl and had a feeling heart.'

'Don't speak so, my child. God has afflicted you sore, and your hardness of heart is but for a time. Wait a little. Don't reproach yourself, my poor Nest. I understand your ways. I don't mind them, love. The feeling heart will come back to you in time. Anyways, don't think you're grieving me, because, love, that may sting you when I'm gone; and I'm not grieved, my darling. Most times we're very cheerful, I think.'

After this, mother, and child were drawn more together. But Eleanor had received her death from these sorrowful, hurrying events. She did not conceal the truth from herself; nor did she pray to live, as some months ago she had done, for her child's sake; she had found out that she had no power to console the poor wounded heart. It seemed to her as if her prayers had been of no avail; and then she blamed herself for this thought.

There are many Methodist preachers in this part of Wales. There was a certain old man, named David Hughes, who was held in peculiar reverence because he had known the great John Wesley. He had been captain of a Caernarvon slate-vessel; he had traded in the Mediterranean, and had seen strange sights. In those early days (to use his own expression) he had lived without God in the world; but he went to mock John Wesley, and was converted by the white-haired patriach, and remained to pray. Afterwards he became one of the earnest, self-denying, much-abused band of itinerant preachers who went forth under Wesley's direction, to spread abroad a more earnest and practical spirit of religion. His rambles, and travels were of use to him. They extended his know-ledge of the circumstances in which men are sometimes placed, and enlarged his sympathy with the tried and tempted. His sympathy, combined with the thoughtful experience of fourscore years, made him cognisant of many of the strange secrets of humanity; and when younger preachers upbraided the hard hearts they met with, and despaired of the sinners, he 'suffered long, and was kind.'

When Eleanor Gwynn lay low on her death-bed, David Hughes came to Pen-Morfa. He knew her history, and sought her out. To him she imparted the feelings I have described.

'I have lost my faith, David. The tempter has come, and I have yielded. I doubt if my prayers have been heard. Day, and night have I prayed that I might comfort my child in her great sorrow; but God has not heard me. She has turned away from me, and refused my poor love. I wish to die now; but I have lost my faith, and have no more pleasure in the thought of going to God. What must I do, David?'

She hung upon his answer; and it was long in coming.

'I am weary of earth,' said she, mournfully, 'and can I find rest in death even, leaving my child desolate and broken-hearted?'

'Eleanor,' said David, 'where you go all things will be made clear; and you will learn to thank God for the end of what now seems grievous and heavy to be borne. Do you think your agony has been greater than the awful agony in the Garden – or your prayers more earnest than that which He prayed in that hour when the great drops of blood ran down his face like sweat? We know that God heard Him, although no answer came to Him through the dread silence of that night. God's times are not our times. I have lived eighty and one years, and never yet have I known an earnest prayer fall to the ground unheeded. In an unknown way, and when no one looked for it, may be, the answer came; a fuller, more satisfying answer than heart could conceive of, although it might be different to what was expected. Sister you are going where in His light you will see light; you will learn there that in very faithfulness he has afflicted you!'

'Go on – you strengthen me,' said she.

After David Hughes left that day, Eleanor was calm as one already dead, and past mortal strife. Nest was awed by the change. No more passionate weeping – no more sorrow in the voice;

though it was low and weak, it sounded with a sweet composure. Her last look was a smile; her last word a blessing.

Nest, tearless, streeked the poor worn body. She laid a plate with salt upon it on the breast, and lighted candles for the head and feet. It was an old Welsh custom; but when David Hughes came in, the sight carried him back to the time when he had seen the chapels in some old Catholic cathedral. Nest sat gazing on the dead with dry, hot eyes.

'She is dead,' said David, solemnly, 'she died in Christ. Let us bless God, my child. He giveth and He taketh away.'

'She is dead,' said Nest, 'my mother is dead. No one loves me now.'

She spoke as if she were thinking aloud, for she did not look at David, or ask him to be seated.

'No one loves you now? No human creature, you mean. You are not yet fit to be spoken to concerning God's infinite love. I, like you, will speak of love for human creatures. I tell you if no one loves you, it is time for you to begin to love.' He spoke almost severely (if David Hughes ever did); for, to tell the truth, he was repelled by her hard rejection of her mother's tenderness, about which the neighbours had told him.

'Begin to love!' said she, her eyes flashing. 'Have I not loved? Old man, you are dim, and worn-out. You do not remember what love is.' She spoke with a scornful kind of pitying endurance. 'I will tell you how I have loved by telling you the change it has wrought in me. I was once the beautiful Nest Gwynn; I am now a cripple, a poor, wan-faced cripple, old before my time. That is a change; at least people think so.' She paused and then spoke lower. 'I tell you, David Hughes, that outward change is as nothing compared to the change in my nature caused by the love I have felt – and have had rejected. I was gentle once, and if you spoke a tender word, my heart came towards you as natural as a little child goes to its mammy. I never spoke roughly, even to the dumb creatures, for I had a kind feeling for all. Of late (since I loved, old man), I have been cruel in my thoughts to every one. I have turned away from tenderness with bitter indifference, Listen!' she spoke in a hoarse whisper. 'I will own it. I have spoken hardly to her,' pointing towards the corpse. 'Her who was ever patient, and full of love for me. She did not know,' she muttered, 'she is gone to the grave without knowing how I loved her – I had such strange, mad, stubborn pride in me.'

'Come back, mother! Come back,' said she, crying wildly to the still, solemn corpse; 'come back as a spirit or a ghost – only come back, that I may tell you how I have loved you.'

But the dead never come back.

The passionate adjuration ended in tears – the first she had shed. When they ceased, or were absorbed into long quivering sobs, David knelt down. Nest did not kneel, but bowed her head. He prayed, while his own tears fell fast. He rose up. They were both calm.

'Nest,' said he, 'your love has been the love of youth; passionate, wild, natural to youth. Henceforward you must love like Christ; without thought of self, or wish for return. You must take the sick and the weary to your heart, and love them. That love will lift you up above the storms of the world into God's own peace. The very vehemence of your nature proves that you are capable of this. I do not pity you. You no not require pity. You are powerful enough to trample down your own sorrows into a blessing for others; and to others you will be a blessing; I see it before you; I see in it the answer to your mother's prayer.'

The old man's dim eyes glittered as if they saw a vision; the fire-light sprang up, and glinted on his long white hair. Nest was awed as if she saw a prophet, and a prophet he was to her.

When next David Hughes came to Pen-Morfa, he asked about Nest Gwynn with a hovering doubt as to the answer. The inn-folk told him she was living still in the cottage, which was now her own.

'But would you believe it, David,' said Mrs Thomas, 'she has gone and taken Mary Williams to live with her? You remember Mary Williams, I'm sure.'

No! David Hughes remembered no Mary Williams at Pen-Morfa.

'You must have seen her, for I know you've called at Thomas Griffiths', where the parish boarded her?'

'You don't mean the half-witted woman – the poor crazy creature?'

'But I do!' said Mrs Thomas.

'I have seen her sure enough, but I never thought of learning her name. And Nest Gwynn has taken her to live with her.'

'Yes! I thought I should surprise you. She might have had many a decent girl for companion. My own niece, her that is an orphan, would have gone, and been thankful. Besides, Mary Williams is a regular savage at times; John Griffiths says there were days when he used to beat her till she howled again, and yet she would not do as he told her. Nay, once, he says, if he had not seen her eyes glare like a wild beast, from under the shadow of the table where she had taken shelter, and got pretty quickly out of her way, she would have flown upon him, and throttled him. He gave Nest fair warning of what she must expect, and he thinks some day she will be found murdered.'

David Hughes thought awhile. 'How came Nest to take her to live with her?' asked he.

'Well! Folk say John Griffiths did not give her enough to eat. Half-wits, they tell me, take more to feed them than others, and Eleanor Gwynn had given her oat-cake, and porridge a time or two, and most likely spoken kindly to her (you know Eleanor spoke kind to all), so some months ago, when John Griffiths had been beating her, and keeping her without food to try, and tame her, she ran away, and came to Nest's cottage in the dead of night, all shivering, and starved, for she did not know Eleanor was dead, and thought to meet with kindness from her, I've no doubt; and Nest remembered how her mother used to feed and comfort the poor idiot, and made her some gruel, and wrapped her up by the fire. And in the morning when John Griffiths came in search of Mary, he found her with Nest, and Mary wailed so piteously at the sight of him, that Nest went to the parish officers, and offered to take her to board with her for the same money they gave to him. John says he was right glad to be off his bargain.'

David Hughes knew there was a kind of remorse which sought relief in the performance of the most difficult and repugnant tasks. He thought he could understand how, in her bitter repentance for her conduct towards her mother, Nest had taken in the first helpless creature that came seeking shelter in her name. It was not what he would have chosen, but he knew it was God that had sent the poor wandering idiot there.

He went to see Nest the next morning. As he drew near the cottage – it was summer time, and the doors and windows were all open – he heard an angry passionate kind of sound that was scarcely human. That sound prevented his approach from being heard; and standing at the threshold, he saw poor Mary Williams pacing backwards, and forwards in some wild mood. Nest, cripple as she was, was walking with her, speaking low soothing words, till the pace was slackened, and time and breathing was

given to put her arm around the crazy woman's neck, and soothe
her by this tender caress into the quiet luxury of tears; tears which
give the hot brain relief. Then David Hughes came in. His first
words, as he took off his hat, standing on the lintel, were – 'The
peace of God be upon this house.' Neither he nor Nest recurred to
the past; though solemn recollections filled their minds. Before he
went, all three knelt and prayed; for, as Nest told him, some
mysterious influence of peace came over the poor half-wit's mind,
when she heard the holy words of prayer; and often when she felt a
paroxysm coming on, she would kneel and repeat a homily
rapidly over, as if it were a charm to scare away the Demon in
possession; sometimes, indeed, the control over herself requisite
for this effort was enough to dispel the fluttering burst. When
David rose up to go, he drew Nest to the door.

'You are not afraid, my child?' asked he.

'No,' she replied. 'She is often very good and quiet. When she is
not, I can bear it.'

'I shall see your face on earth no more;' said he. 'God bless you!'
He went on his way. Not many weeks after, David Hughes was
borne to his grave.

The doors of Nest's heart were opened – opened wide by the
love she grew to feel for crazy Mary, so helpless, so friendless, so
dependent upon her. Mary loved her back again, as a dumb animal
loves its blind master. It was happiness enough to be near her. In
general she was only too glad to do what she was bidden by Nest.
But there were times when Mary was overpowered by the glooms
and fancies of her poor disordered brain. Fearful times! No one
knew how fearful. On those days, Nest warned the little children
who loved to come, and play around her, that they must not visit
the house. The signal was a piece of white linen hung out of a
side-window. On those days the sorrowful, and sick waited in
vain for the sound of Nest's lame approach. But what she had to
endure was only known to God, for she never complained. If she
had given up the charge of Mary, or if the neighbours had risen out
of love, and care for her life, to compel such a step, she knew what
hard curses and blows – what starvation and misery, would await
the poor creature.

She told of Mary's docility, and her affection, and her innocent
little sayings; but she never told the details of the occasional days
of wild disorder, and driving insanity.

Nest grew old before her time, in consequence of her accident.

She knew that she was as old at fifty as many are at seventy. She knew it partly by the vividness with which the remembrance of the days of her youth came back to her mind, while the events of yesterday were dim, and forgotten. She dreamt of her girlhood, and youth. In sleep she was once more the beautiful Nest Gwynn, the admired of all beholders, the light-hearted girl, beloved by her mother. Little circumstances connected with those early days, forgotten since the very time when they occurred, came back to her mind, in her waking hours. She had a scar on the palm of her left hand, occasioned by the fall of a branch of a tree, when she was a child; it had not pained her since the first two days after the accident; but now it began to hurt her slightly; and clear in her ears was the crackling sound of the treacherous, rending wood; distinct before her rose the presence of her mother tenderly binding up the wound. With these remembrances came a longing desire to see the beautiful fatal well, once more before her death. She had never gone so far since the day when, by her fall there, she lost love, and hope, and her bright glad youth. She yearned to look upon its waters once again. This desire waxed as her life waxed. She told it to poor crazy Mary.

'Mary!' said she, 'I want to go to the Rock Well. If you will help me, I can manage it. There used to be many a stone in the Dol Mawr on which I could sit and rest. We will go to-morrow morning before folks are astir.'

Mary answered briskly, 'Up, up! To the Rock Well: Mary will go. Mary will go.' All day long she kept muttering to herself, 'Mary will go.'

Nest had the happiest dream that night. Her mother stood beside her – not in the flesh, but in the bright glory of a blessed spirit. And Nest was no longer young – neither was she old – 'they reckon not by days, nor years where she was gone to dwell;' and her mother stretched out her arms to her with a calm glad look of welcome. She awoke; the woodlark was singing in the near copse – the little birds were astir, and rustling in their leafy nests. Nest arose, and called Mary. The two set out through the quiet lane. They went along slowly, and silently. With many a pause they crossed the broad Dol Mawr; and carefully descended the sloping stones, on which no trace remained of the hundreds of feet that had passed over them since Nest was last there. The clear water sparkled and quivered in the early sun-light, the shadows of the birch-leaves were stirred on the ground; the ferns – Nest could have believed that they were the very same ferns which she had seen thirty years before, hung wet and dripping where the water over-flowed – a thrush chanted matins from a holly bush near – and the running stream made a low, soft, sweet accompaniment. All was the same; Nature was as fresh and young as ever. It might have been yesterday that Edward Williams had overtaken her, and told her his love – the thought of his words – his handsome looks – (he was a grey hard-featured man by this time), and then she recalled the fatal wintry morning when joy, and youth had fled; and as she remembered that faintness of pain, a new, a real faintness – no echo of the memory – came over her. She leant her back against a rock, without a moan or sigh, and died! She found immortality by the well side, instead of her fragile perishing youth. She was so calm, and placid that Mary (who had been dipping her fingers in the well, to see the waters drop off in the gleaming sun-light), thought she was asleep, and for some time continued her amusement in silence. At last she turned, and said,

'Mary is tired. Mary wants to go home.' Nest did not speak, though the idiot repeated her plaintive words. She stood and looked till a strange terror came over her – a terror too mysterious to be borne.

'Mistress, wake! Mistress, wake!' she said, wildly, shaking the form.

But Nest did not awake. And the first person who came to the well that morning found crazy Mary sitting, awe-struck, by the poor dead Nest. They had to get the poor creature away by force, before they could remove the body.

Mary is in Trê-Madoc workhouse; they treat her pretty kindly, and in general she is good and tractable. Occasionally the old paroxysms come on; and for a time she is unmanageable. But some one thought of speaking to her about Nest. She stood arrested at the name; and since then, it is astonishing to see what efforts she makes to curb her insanity; and when the dread time is past, she creeps up to the matron, and says, 'Mary has tried to be good. Will God let her go to Nest now?'

THE MANCHESTER
MARRIAGE

Mr and Mrs Openshaw came from Manchester to settle in London. He had been, what is called in Lancashire, a salesman for a large manufacturing firm, who were extending their business, and opening a warehouse in the city; where Mr Openshaw was now to superintend their affairs. He rather enjoyed the change; having a kind of curiosity about London, which he had never yet been able to gratify in his brief visits to the metropolis. At the same time, he had an odd, shrewd contempt for the inhabitants, whom he always pictured to himself as fine, lazy people, caring nothing but for fashion and aristocracy, and lounging away their days in Bond Street, and such places; ruining good English, and ready in their turn to despise him as a provincial. The hours that the men of business kept in the city scandalized him too, accustomed as he was to the early dinners of Manchester folk and the consequently far longer evenings. Still, he was pleased to go to London, though he would not for the world have confessed it, even to himself, and always spoke of the step to his friends as one demanded of him by the interests of his employers, and sweetened to him by a considerable increase of salary. This, indeed, was so liberal that he might have been justified in taking a much larger house than the one he did, had he not thought himself bound to set an example to Londoners of how little a Manchester man of business cared for show. Inside, however, he furnished it with an unusual degree of comfort, and, in the winter-time, he insisted on keeping up as large fires as the grates would allow, in every room where the temperature was in the least chilly. Moreover, his northern sense of hospitality was such that, if he were at home, he could hardly suffer a visitor to leave the house without forcing meat and drink upon him. Every servant in the house was well warmed, well fed, and kindly treated; for their master scorned all petty saving in aught that conduced to comfort; while he amused himself by following out all his accustomed habits and individuals ways, in defiance of what any of his new neighbours might think.

His wife was a pretty, gentle woman, of suitable age and character. He was forty-two, she thirty-five. He was loud and decided; she soft and yielding. They had two children; or rather, I should say, she had two; for the elder, a girl of eleven, was Mrs Openshaw's child by Frank Wilson, her first husband. The younger was a little boy, Edwin, who could just prattle, and to whom his father delighted to speak in the broadest and most unintelligible Lancashire dialect, in order to keep up what he called the true Saxon accent.

Mrs Openshaw's Christian name was Alice, and her first husband had been her own cousin. She was the orphan niece of a sea-captain in Liverpool; a quiet, grave little creature, of great personal attraction when she was fifteen or sixteen, with regular features and a blooming complexion. But she was very shy, and believed herself to be very stupid and awkward; and was frequently scolded by her aunt, her own uncle's second wife. So when her cousin, Frank Wilson, came home from a long absence at sea, and first was kind and protective to her; secondly, attentive; and thirdly, desperately in love with her, she hardly knew how to be grateful enough to him. It is true, she would have preferred his remaining in the first or second stages of behaviour; for his violent love puzzled and frightened her. Her uncle neither helped nor hindered the love affair, though it was going on under his own eyes. Frank's stepmother had such a variable temper, that there was no knowing whether what she liked one day she would like the next, or not. At length she went to such extremes of crossness that Alice was only too glad to shut her eyes and rush blindly at the chance of escape from domestic tyranny offered her by a marriage with her cousin; and, liking him better than any one in the world, except her uncle (who was at this time at sea), she went off one morning and was married to him, her only bridesmaid being the housemaid at her aunt's. The consequence was that Frank and his wife went into lodgings, and Mrs Wilson refused to see them, and turned away Norah, the warm-hearted housemaid, whom they accordingly took into their service. When Captain Wilson returned from his voyage he was very cordial with the young couple, and spent many an evening at their lodgings, smoking his pipe and sipping his grog; but he told them, for quietness' sake, he could not ask them to his own house; for his wife was bitter against them. They were not, however, very unhappy about this.

The seed of future unhappiness lay rather in Frank's vehement, passionate disposition, which led him to resent his wife's shyness and want of demonstrativeness as failures in conjugal duty. He was already tormenting himself, and her too in a slighter degree, by apprehensions and imaginations of what might befall her during his approaching absence at sea. At last, he went to his father and urged him to insist upon Alice's being once more received under his roof; the more especially as there was now a prospect of her confinement while her husband was away on his voyage. Captain Wilson was, as he himself expressed it, 'breaking up,' and unwilling to undergo the excitement of a scene; yet he felt that what his son said was true. So he went to his wife. And before Frank set sail, he had the comfort of seeing his wife installed in her old little garret in his father's house. To have placed her in the one best spare room was a step beyond Mrs Wilson's powers of submission or generosity. The worst part about it, however, was that the faithful Norah had to be dismissed. Her place as house-maid had been filled up; and, even if it had not, she had forfeited Mrs Wilson's good opinion for ever. She comforted her young master and mistress by pleasant prophecies of the time when they would have a household of their own; of which, whatever service she might be in meanwhile, she should be sure to form a part. Almost the last action Frank did, before setting sail, was going with Alice to see Norah once more at her mother's house; and then he went away.

Alice's father-in-law grew more and more feeble as winter advanced. She was of great use to her stepmother in nursing and amusing him; and although there was anxiety enough in the household, there was, perhaps, more of peace than there had been for years, for Mrs Wilson had not a bad heart, and was softened by the visible approach of death to one whom she loved, and touched by the lonely condition of the young creature expecting her first confinement in her husband's absence. To this relenting mood Norah owed the permission to come and nurse Alice when her baby was born, and to remain and attend on Captain Wilson.

Before one letter had been received from Frank (who had sailed for the East Indies and China), his father died. Alice was always glad to remember that he had held her baby in his arms, and kissed and blessed it before his death. After that, and the consequent examination into the state of his affairs, it was found that he had left far less property than people had been led by his style of living to expect; and what money there was, was settled all upon his wife, and at her disposal after her death. This did not signify much to Alice, as Frank was now first mate of his ship, and, in another voyage or two, would be captain. Meanwhile he had left her rather more than two hundred pounds (all his savings) in the bank.

It became time for Alice to hear from her husband. One letter from the Cape she had already received. The next was to announce his arrival in India. As week after week passed over, and no intelligence of the ship having got there reached the office of the owners, and the captain's wife was in the same state of ignorant suspense as Alice herself, her fears grew most oppressive. At length the day came when, in reply to her inquiry at the shipping office, they told her that the owners had given up hope of ever hearing more of the *Betsy-Jane*, and had sent in their claim upon the underwriters. Now that he was gone for ever, she first felt a yearning, longing love for the kind cousin, the dear friend, the sympathizing protector, whom she should never see again; – first felt a passionate desire to show him his child, whom she had hitherto rather craved to have all to herself – her own sole possession. Her grief was, however, noiseless and quiet – rather to the scandal of Mrs Wilson who bewailed her stepson as if he and she had always lived together in perfect harmony, and who evidently thought it her duty to burst into fresh tears at every strange face she saw; dwelling on his poor young widow's desolate state, and the helplessness of the fatherless child, with an unction as if she liked the excitement of the sorrowful story.

So passed away the first days of Alice's widowhood. By and by things subsided into their natural and tranquil course. But, as if the young creature was always to be in some heavy trouble, her ewe-lamb began to be ailing, pining, and sickly. The child's mysterious illness turned out to be some affection of the spine, likely to affect health but not to shorten life – at least, so the doctors said. But the long, dreary suffering of one whom a mother loves as Alice loved her only child, is hard to look forward to. Only Norah guessed what Alice suffered; no one but God knew.

And so it fell out, that when Mrs Wilson, the elder, came to her one day, in violent distress, occasioned by a very material diminution in the value of the property that her husband had left her – a diminution which made her income barely enough to support herself, much less Alice – the latter could hardly understand how anything which did not touch health or life could cause such grief;

and she received the intelligence with irritating composure. But when, that afternoon, the little sick child was brought in, and the grandmother – who, after all, loved it well – began a fresh moan over her losses to its unconscious ears – saying how she had planned to consult this or that doctor, and to give it this or that comfort or luxury in after years, but that now all chance of this had passed away – Alice's heart was touched, and she drew near to Mrs Wilson with unwonted caresses, and, in a spirit not unlike to that of Ruth, entreated that, come what would, they might remain together. After much discussion in succeeding days, it was arranged that Mrs Wilson should take a house in Manchester, furnishing it partly with what furniture she had, and providing the rest with Alice's remaining two hundred pounds. Mrs Wilson was herself a Manchester woman, and naturally longed to return to her native town; some connexions of her own, too, at that time required lodgings, for which they were willing to pay pretty handsomely. Alice undertook the active superintendence and superior work of the household; Norah – willing, faithful Norah – offered to cook, scour, do anything in short, so that she might but remain with them.

The plan succeeded. For some years their first lodgers remained with them, and all went smoothly – with the one sad exception of the little girl's increasing deformity. How that mother loved that child, it is not for words to tell!

Then came a break of misfortune. Their lodgers left, and no one succeeded to them. After some months, it became necessary to remove to a smaller house; and Alice's tender conscience was torn by the idea that she ought not to be a burden to her mother-in-law, but to go out and seek her own maintenance. And leave her child! The thought came like the sweeping boom of a funeral-bell over her heart.

By and by, Mr Openshaw came to lodge with them. He had started in life as the errand-boy and sweeper-out of a warehouse; had struggled up through all the grades of employment in it, fighting his way through the hard, striving Manchester life with strong, pushing energy of character. Every spare moment of time had been sternly given up to self-teaching. He was a capital accountant, a good French and German scholar, a keen, far-seeing tradesman – understanding markets and the bearing of events, both near and distant, on trade; and yet, with such vivid attention to present details, that I do not think he ever saw a group of flowers in the fields without thinking whether their colour would, or would not, form harmonious contrasts in the coming spring muslins and prints. He went to debating societies, and threw himself with all his heart and soul into politics; esteeming, it must be owned, every man a fool or a knave who differed from him, and overthrowing his opponents rather by the loud strength of his language than the calm strength of his logic. There was something of the Yankee in all this. Indeed, his theory ran parallel to the famous Yankee motto – 'England flogs creation, and Manchester flogs England.' Such a man, as may be fancied, had had no time for falling in love, or any such nonsense. At the age when most young men go through their courting and matrimony, he had not the means of keeping a wife, and was far too practical to think of having one. And now that he was in easy circumstances, a rising man, he considered women almost as encumbrances to the world, with whom a man had better have as little to do as possible. His first impression of Alice was indistinct, and he did not care enough about her to make it distinct. 'A pretty, yea-nay kind of woman,' would have been his description of her, if he had been pushed into a corner. He was rather afraid, in the beginning, that her quiet ways arose from a listlessness and laziness of character, which would have been exceedingly discordant to his active, energetic nature. But, when he found out the punctuality with which his wishes were attended to, and her work was done; when he was called in the morning at the very stroke of the clock, his shaving-water scalding hot, his fire bright, his coffee made exactly as his peculiar fancy dictated (for he was a man who had his theory about everything based upon what he knew of science, and often perfectly original) – then he began to think: not that Alice had any particular merit, but that he had got into remarkably good lodgings; his restlessness wore away, and he began to consider himself as almost settled for life in them.

Mr Openshaw had been too busy, all his days, to be introspective. He did not know that he had any tenderness in his nature; and if he had become conscious of its abstract existence he would have considered it as a manifestation of disease in some part of him. But he was decoyed into pity unawares; and pity led on to tenderness. That little helpless child – always carried about by one of the three busy women of the house, or else patiently threading coloured beads in the chair from which, by no effort of its own, could it ever move – the great grave blue eyes, full of serious, not uncheerful, expression, giving to the small delicate face a look beyond its years – the soft plaintive voice dropping out but few words, so unlike the continual prattle of a child – caught Mr Openshaw's attention in spite of himself. One day – he half scorned himself for doing so – he cut short his dinner-hour to go in search of some toy, which should take the place of those eternal beads. I forget what he bought; but, when he gave the present (which he took care to do in a short abrupt manner, and when no one was by to see him), he was almost thrilled by the flash of delight that came over that child's face, and he could not help, all through that afternoon, going over and over again the picture left on his memory, by the bright effect of unexpected joy on the little girl's face. When he returned home, he found his slippers placed by his sitting-room fire; and even more careful attention paid to his fancies than was habitual in those model lodgings. When Alice had taken the last of his tea-things away – she had been silent as usual till then – she stood for an instant with the door in her hand. Mr Openshaw looked as if he were deep in his book, though in fact he did not see a line; but was heartily wishing the woman would go, and not make any palaver of gratitude. But she only said:

'I am very much obliged to you, sir. Thank you very much,' and was gone, even before he could send her away with a 'There, my good woman, that's enough!'

For some time longer he took no apparent notice of the child. He even hardened his heart into disregarding her sudden flush of colour and little timid smile of recognition, when he saw her by chance. But, after all, this could not last for ever; and, having a second time given way to tenderness, there was no relapse. The insidious enemy having thus entered his heart, in the guise of compassion to the child, soon assumed the more dangerous form of interest in the mother. He was aware of this change of feeling – despised himself for it – struggled with it; nay, internally yielded to it and cherished it, long before he suffered the slightest expression of it, by word, action, or look to escape him. He watched Alice's docile, obedient ways to her stepmother; the love which she had inspired in the rough Norah (roughened by the wear and tear of sorrow and years); but, above all, he saw the wild, deep, passionate affection existing between her and her child. They spoke little to any one else, or when any one else was by; but, when alone together, they talked, and murmured, and cooed, and chattered so continually, that Mr Openshaw first wondered what they could find to say to each other, and next became irritated because they were always so grave and silent with him. All this time he was perpetually devising small new pleasures for the child. His thoughts ran, in a pertinacious way, upon the desolate life before her; and often he came back from his day's work loaded with the very thing Alice had been longing for, but had not been able to procure. One time, it was a little chair for drawing the little sufferer along the streets; and, many an evening that following summer, Mr Openshaw drew her along himself, regardless of the remarks of his acquaintances. One day in autumn, he put down his newspaper, as Alice came in with the breakfast, and said, in as indifferent a voice as he could assume:

'Mrs Frank, is there any reason why we two should not put up our horses together?'

Alice stood still in perplexed wonder. What did he mean? He had resumed the reading of his newspaper, as if he did not expect any answer; so she found silence her safest course, and went on quietly arranging his breakfast, without another word passing between them. Just as he was leaving the house, to go to the warehouse as usual, he turned back and put his head into the bright, neat, tidy kitchen, where all the women breakfasted in the morning:

'You'll think of what I said, Mrs Frank' (this was her name with the lodgers), 'and let me have your opinion upon it to-night.'

Alice was thankful that her mother and Norah were too busy talking together to attend much to this speech. She determined not to think about it at all through the day; and, of course, the effort not to think made her think all the more. At night she sent up Norah with his tea. But Mr Openshaw almost knocked Norah down as she was going out at the door, by pushing past her and calling out, 'Mrs Frank!' in an impatient voice, at the top of the stairs.

Alice went up, rather than seem to have affixed too much meaning to his words.

'Well, Mrs Frank,' he said, 'what answer? Don't make it too long; for I have lots of office work to get through to-night.'

'I hardly know what you meant, sir,' said truthful Alice.

'Well! I should have thought you might have guessed. You're not new at this sort of work, and I am. However, I'll make it plain this time. Will you have me to be thy wedded husband, and serve me, and love me, and honour me, and all that sort of thing? Because, if you will, I will do as much by you, and be a father to your child – and that's more than is put in the Prayer-book. Now, I'm a man of my word; and what I say, I feel; and what I promise, I'll do. Now, for your answer!'

Alice was silent. He began to make the tea, as if her reply was a matter of perfect indifference to him; but, as soon as that was done, he became impatient.

'Well?' said he.

'How long, sir, may I have to think over it?'

'Three minutes!' (looking at his watch). 'You've had two already – that makes five. Be a sensible woman, say Yes, and sit down to tea with me, and we'll talk it over together; for, after tea, I shall be busy; say No' (he hesitated a moment to try and keep his voice in the same tone), 'and I shan't say another word about it, but pay up a year's rent for my rooms to-morrow, and be off. Time's up! Yes or no?'

'If you please, sir – you have been so good to little Ailsie – '

'There, sit down comfortably by me on the sofa, and let's have our tea together. I am glad to find you are as good and sensible as I took you for.'

And this was Alice Wilson's second wooing.

Mr Openshaw's will was too strong, and his circumstances too good, for him not to carry all before him. He settled Mrs Wilson in a comfortable house of her own, and made her quite independent of lodgers. The little that Alice said with regard to future plans was in Norah's behalf.

'No,' said Mr Openshaw. 'Norah shall take care of the old lady as long as she lives; and, after that, she shall either come and live with us, or, if she likes it better, she shall have a provision for life – for your sake, missus. No one who has been good to you or the child shall go unrewarded. But even the little one will be better for some fresh stuff about her. Get her a bright, sensible girl as a nurse; one who won't go rubbing her with calf's-foot jelly as Norah does; wasting good stuff outside that ought to go in, but will follow doctors' directions; which, as you must see pretty clearly by this time, Norah won't; because they give the poor little wench pain. Now, I'm not above being nesh for other folks myself. I can stand a good blow, and never change colour; but, set me in the operating room in the infirmary, and I turn as sick as a girl. Yet, if need were, I would hold the little wench on my knees while she screeched with pain, if it were to do her poor back good. Nay, nay, wench! keep your white looks for the time when it comes – I don't say it ever will. But this I know, Norah will spare the child and cheat the doctor, if she can. Now, I say, give the bairn a year or two's chance, and then, when the pack of doctors have done their best – and, maybe, the old lady has gone – we'll have Norah back or do better for her.'

The pack of doctors could do no good to little Ailsie. She was beyond their power. But her father (for so he insisted on being called, and also on Alice's no longer retaining the appellation of Mamma, but becoming henceforward Mother), by his healthy cheerfulness of manner, his clear decision of purpose, his odd turns and quirks of humour, added to his real strong love for the helpless little girl, infused a new element of brightness and confidence into her life; and, though her back remained the same, her general health was strengthened, and Alice – never going beyond a smile herself – had the pleasure of seeing her child taught to laugh.

As for Alice's own life, it was happier than it had ever been before. Mr Openshaw required no demonstration, no expressions of affection from her. Indeed, these would rather have disgusted him. Alice could love deeply, but could not talk about it. The perpetual requirement of loving words, looks, and caresses, and misconstruing their absence into absence of love, had been the great trial of her former married life. Now, all went on clear and straight, under the guidance of her husband's strong sense, warm heart, and powerful will. Year by year their worldly prosperity increased. At Mrs Wilson's death, Norah came back to them as nurse to the newly-born little Edwin; into which post she was not installed without a pretty strong oration on the part of the proud and happy father, who declared that if he found out that Norah ever tried to screen the boy by a falsehood, or to make him nesh either in body or mind, she should go that very day. Norah and Mr Openshaw were not on the most thoroughly cordial terms; neither of them fully recognizing or appreciating the other's best qualities.

This was the previous history of the Lancashire family who had now removed to London.

They had been there about a year, when Mr Openshaw suddenly informed his wife that he had determined to heal long-standing feuds, and had asked his uncle and aunt Chadwick to come and pay them a visit and see London. Mrs Openshaw had never seen this uncle and aunt of her husband's. Years before she had married him, there had been a quarrel. All she knew was, that Mr Chadwick was a small manufacturer in a country town in South Lancashire. She was extremely pleased that the breach was to be healed, and began making preparations to render their visit pleasant.

They arrived at last. Going to see London was such an event to them, that Mrs Chadwick had made all new linen fresh for the occasion – from night-caps downwards; and as for gowns, ribbons, and collars, she might have been going into the wilds of Canada where never a shop is, so large was her stock. A fortnight before the day of her departure for London, she had formally called to take leave of all her acquaintance; saying she should need every bit of the intermediate time for packing up. It was like a second wedding in her imagination; and, to complete the resemblance which an entirely new wardrobe made between the two events, her husband brought her back from Manchester, on the last market-day before they set off, a gorgeous pearl and amethyst brooch, saying, 'Lunnon should see that Lancashire folks knew a handsome thing when they saw it.'

For some time after Mr and Mrs Chadwick arrived at the Openshaws' there was no opportunity for wearing this brooch; but at length they obtained an order to see Buckingham Palace, and the spirit of loyalty demanded that Mrs Chadwick should wear her best clothes in visiting the abode of her sovereign. On her return she hastily changed her dress; for Mr Openshaw had planned that they should go to Richmond, drink tea, and return by moonlight. Accordingly, about five o'clock, Mr and Mrs Openshaw and Mr and Mrs Chadwick set off.

The housemaid and cook sat below, Norah hardly knew where. She was always engrossed in the nursery in tending her two children, and in sitting by the restless, excitable Ailsie till she fell asleep. By and by the housemaid Bessy tapped gently at the door. Norah went to her, and they spoke in whispers.

'Nurse! there's some one downstairs wants you.'

'Wants me! who is it?'

'A gentleman – '

'A gentleman? Nonsense!'

'Well! a man, then, and he asks for you, and he rang at the front-door bell, and has walked into the dining-room.'

'You should never have let him,' exclaimed Norah. 'Master and missus out – '

'I did not want him to come in; but, when he heard you lived here, he walked past me, and sat down on the first chair, and said, "Tell her to come and speak to me." There is no gas lighted in the room, and supper is all set out.'

'He'll be off with the spoons!' exclaimed Norah, putting the housemaid's fear into words, and preparing to leave the room; first, however, giving a look to Ailsie, sleeping soundly and calmly.

Downstairs she went, uneasy fears stirring in her bosom. Before she entered the dining-room she provided herself with a candle, and, with it in her hand, she went in, looking around her in the darkness for her visitor.

He was standing up, holding by the table. Norah and he looked at each other; gradual recognition coming into their eyes.

'Norah?' at length he asked.

'Who are you?' asked Norah, with the sharp tones of alarm and incredulity. 'I don't know you'; trying, by futile words of disbelief, to do away with the terrible fact before her.

'Am I so changed?' he said pathetically. 'I dare say I am. But, Norah, tell me!' he breathed hard, 'where is my wife? Is she – is she alive?'

He came nearer to Norah, and would have taken her hand; but she backed away from him; looking at him all the time with staring eyes, as if he were some horrible object. Yet he was a handsome, bronzed, good-looking fellow, with beard and moustache, giving him a foreign-looking aspect; but his eyes! there was no mistaking those eager, beautiful eyes – the very same that Norah had watched not half an hour ago, till sleep stole softly over them.

'Tell me, Norah – I can bear it – I have feared it so often. Is she dead?' Norah still kept silence. 'She is dead!' He hung on Norah's words and looks, as if for confirmation or contradiction.

'What shall I do?' groaned Norah. 'Oh, sir! why did you come? how did you find me out? where have you been? We thought you dead, we did indeed!' She poured out words and questions to gain time, as if time would help her.

'Norah! answer me this question straight, by yes or no – Is my wife dead?'

'No, she is not?' said Norah, slowly and heavily.

'Oh, what a relief! Did she receive my letters? But perhaps you don't know. Why did you leave her? Where is she? Oh, Norah, tell me all quickly!'

'Mr Frank!' said Norah at last, almost driven to bay by her terror lest her mistress should return at any moment and find him there – unable to consider what was best to be done or said – rushing at something decisive, because she could not endure her present state: 'Mr Frank! we never heard a line from you, and the shipowners said you had gone down, you and every one else. We thought you were dead, if ever man was, and poor Miss Alice and her little sick, helpless child! Oh, sir, you must guess it,' cried the poor creature at last, bursting out into a passionate fit of crying, 'for indeed I cannot tell it. But it was no one's fault. God help us all this night!'

Norah had sat down. She trembled too much to stand. He took her hands in his. He squeezed them hard, as if, by physical pressure, the truth could be wrung out.

'Norah.' This time his tone was calm, stagnant as despair. 'She has married again!'

Norah shook her head sadly. The grasp slowly relaxed. The man had fainted.

There was brandy in the room. Norah forced some drops into Mr Frank's mouth, chafed his hands, and – when mere animal life returned, before the mind poured in its flood of memories and thoughts – she lifted him up, and rested his head against her knees. Then she put a few crumbs of bread taken from the supper-table, soaked in brandy, into his mouth. Suddenly he sprang to his feet.

'Where is she? Tell me this instant.' He looked so wild, so mad, so desperate, that Norah felt herself to be in bodily danger; but her time of dread had gone by. She had been afraid to tell him the truth, and then she had been a coward. Now, her wits were sharpened by the sense of his desperate state. He must leave the house. She would pity him afterwards; but now she must rather command and upbraid; for he must leave the house before her mistress came home. That one necessity stood clear before her.

'She is not here: that is enough for you to know. Nor can I say exactly where she is' (which was true to the letter if not to the spirit). 'Go away, and tell me where to find you to-morrow, and I will tell you all. My master and mistress may come back at any minute, and then what would become of me, with a strange man in the house?'

Such an argument was too petty to touch his excited mind.

'I don't care for your master and mistress. If your master is a man, he must feel for me – poor shipwrecked sailor that I am – kept for years a prisoner amongst savages, always, always, always thinking of my wife and my home – dreaming of her by night, talking to her though she could not hear, by day. I loved her more than all heaven and earth put together. Tell me where she is, this instant, you wretched woman, who salved over her wickedness to her, as you do to me!'

The clock struck ten. Desperate positions require desperate measures.

'If you will leave the house now, I will come to you to-morrow and tell you all. What is more, you shall see your child now. She lies sleeping upstairs. Oh, sir, you have a child, you do not know that as yet – a little weakly girl – with just a heart and soul beyond her years. We have reared her up with such care! We watched her, for we thought for many a year she might die any day, and we tended her, and no hard thing has come near her, and no rough word has ever been said to her. And now you come and will take her life into your hand, and will crush it. Strangers to her have been kind to her; but her own father – Mr Frank, I am her nurse, and I love her, and I tend her, and I would do anything for her that I could. Her mother's heart beats as hers beats; and, if she suffers a pain, her mother trembles all over. If she is happy, it is her mother that smiles and is glad. If she is growing stronger, her mother is healthy: if she dwindles, her mother languishes. If she dies – well, I don't know; it is not every one can lie down and die when they wish it. Come upstairs, Mr Frank, and see your child. Seeing her will do good to your poor heart. Then go away, in God's name, just this one night; to-morrow, if need be, you can do anything – kill us all if you will, or show yourself a great, grand man, whom God will bless for ever and ever. Come, Mr Frank, the look of a sleeping child is sure to give peace.'

She led him upstairs; at first almost helping his steps, till they came near the nursery door. She had wellnigh forgotten the existence of little Edwin. It struck upon her with affright as the shaded light fell over the other cot; but she skilfully threw that corner of the room into darkness, and let the light fall on the sleeping Ailsie. The child had thrown down the coverings, and her deformity, as she lay with her back to them, was plainly visible through her slight nightgown. Her little face, deprived of the lustre of her eyes, looked wan and pinched, and had a pathetic expression in it, even as she slept. The poor father looked and looked with hungry, wistful eyes, into which the big tears came swelling up slowly and dropped heavily down, as he stood trembling and shaking all over. Norah was angry with herself for growing impatient of the length of time that long lingering gaze lasted. She thought that she waited for full half an hour before Frank stirred. And then – instead of going away – he sank down on his knees by the bedside, and buried his face in the clothes. Little Ailsie stirred uneasily. Norah pulled him up in terror. She could afford no more time, even for prayer, in her extremity of fear; for surely the next moment would bring her mistress home. She took him forcibly by the arm; but, as he was going, his eye lighted on the other bed: he stopped. Intelligence came back into his face. His hands clenched.

'His child?' he asked.

'Her child,' replied Norah. 'God watches over him,' she said instinctively; for Frank's looks excited her fears, and she needed to remind herself of the Protector of the helpless.

'God has not watched over me,' he said, in despair; his thoughts apparently recoiling on his own desolate, deserted state. But Norah had no time for pity. To-morrow she would be as compassionate as her heart prompted. At length she guided him downstairs, and shut the outer door, and bolted it – as if by bolts to keep out facts.

Then she went back into the dining-room, and effaced all traces of his presence, as far as she could. She went upstairs to the nursery and sat there, her head on her hand, thinking what was to come of all this misery. It seemed to her very long before her master and mistress returned; yet it was hardly eleven o'clock. She heard the loud, hearty Lancashire voices on the stairs; and, for the first time, she understood the contrast of the desolation of the poor man who had so lately gone forth in lonely despair.

It almost put her out of patience to see Mrs Openshaw come in, calmly smiling, handsomely dressed, happy, easy, to inquire after her children.

'Did Ailsie go to sleep comfortably?' she whispered to Norah.

'Yes.'

Her mother bent over her, looking at her slumbers with the soft eyes of love. How little she dreamed who had looked on her last! Then she went to Edwin, with perhaps less wistful anxiety in her countenance, but more of pride. She took off her things, to go down to supper. Norah saw her no more that night.

Beside having a door into the passage, the sleeping-nursery opened out of Mr and Mrs Openshaw's room, in order that they might have the children more immediately under their own eyes. Early the next summer's morning, Mrs Openshaw was awakened by Ailsie's startled call of 'Mother! mother!' She sprang up, put on her dressing-gown, and went to her child. Ailsie was only half awake, and in a not unusual state of terror.

'Who was he, mother? Tell me!'

'Who, my darling? No one is here. You have been dreaming, love. Waken up quite. See, it is broad daylight.'

'Yes,' said Ailsie, looking round her; then clinging to her mother, 'but a man was here in the night, mother.'

'Nonsense, little goose. No man has ever come near you!'

'Yes, he did. He stood there. Just by Norah. A man with hair and a beard. And he knelt down and said his prayers. Norah knows he was here, mother' (half angrily, as Mrs Openshaw shook her head in smiling incredulity).

'Well! we will ask Norah when she comes,' said Mrs Openshaw, soothingly. 'But we won't talk any more about him now. It is not five o'clock; it is too early for you to get up. Shall I fetch you a book and read to you?'

'Don't leave me, mother,' said the child, clinging to her. So Mrs Openshaw sat on the bedside talking to Ailsie, and telling her of what they had done at Richmond the evening before, until the little girl's eyes slowly closed and she once more fell asleep.

'What was the matter?' asked Mr Openshaw, as his wife returned to bed.

'Ailsie wakened up in a fright, with some story of a man having been in the room to say his prayers – a dream, I suppose.' And no more was said at the time.

Mrs Openshaw had almost forgotten the whole affair when she got up about seven o'clock. But, by and by, she heard a sharp altercation going on in the nursery – Norah speaking angrily to Ailsie, a most unusual thing. Both Mr and Mrs Openshaw listened in astonishment.

'Hold your tongue, Ailsie! let me hear none of your dreams; never let me hear you tell that story again!'

Ailsie began to cry.

Mr Openshaw opened the door of communication, before his wife could say a word.

'Norah, come here!'

The nurse stood at the door, defiant. She perceived she had been heard, but she was desperate.

'Don't let me hear you speak in that manner to Ailsie again,' he said sternly, and shut the door.

Norah was infinitely relieved; for she had dreaded some questioning; and a little blame for sharp speaking was what she could well bear, if cross-examination was let alone.

Downstairs they went, Mr Openshaw carrying Ailsie; the sturdy Edwin coming step by step, right foot foremost, always holding his mother's hand. Each child was placed in a chair by the breakfast-table, and then Mr and Mrs Openshaw stood together at the window, awaiting their visitors' appearance and making plans for the day. There was a pause. Suddenly Mr Openshaw turned to Ailsie, and said:

'What a little goosy somebody is with her dreams, wakening up poor, tired mother in the middle of the night, with a story of a man being in the room.'

'Father! I'm sure I saw him,' said Ailsie, half-crying. 'I don't want to make Norah angry; but I was not asleep, for all she says I was. I had been asleep – and I wakened up quite wide awake, though I was so frightened. I kept my eyes nearly shut, and I saw the man quite plain. A great brown man with a beard. He said his prayers. And then looked at Edwin. And then Norah took him by the arm and led him away, after they had whispered a bit together.'

'Now, my little woman must be reasonable,' said Mr Openshaw, who was always patient with Ailsie. 'There was no man in the house last night at all. No man comes into the house, as you know, if you think; much less goes up into the nursery. But sometimes we dream something has happened, and the dream is so like reality, that you are not the first person, little woman, who has stood out that the thing has really happened.'

'But, indeed, it was not a dream!' said Ailsie, beginning to cry.

Just then Mr and Mrs Chadwick came down, looking grave and discomposed. All during breakfast-time they were silent and uncomfortable. As soon as the breakfast things were taken away, and the children had been carried upstairs, Mr Chadwick began, in an evidently preconcerted manner, to inquire if his nephew was certain that all his servants were honest; for, that Mrs Chadwick had that morning missed a very valuable brooch, which she had worn the day before. She remembered taking it off when she came home from Buckingham Palace. Mr Openshaw's face contracted into hard lines; grew like what it was before he had known his wife and her child. He rang the bell, even before his uncle had done speaking. It was answered by the housemaid.

'Mary, was any one here last night, while we were away?'

'A man, sir, came to speak to Norah.'

'To speak to Norah! Who was he? How long did he stay?'

'I'm sure I can't tell, sir. He came – perhaps about nine. I went up to tell Norah in the nursery, and she came down to speak to him. She let him out, sir. She will know who he was, and how long he stayed.'

She waited a moment to be asked any more questions, but she was not, so she went away.

A minute afterwards Mr Openshaw made as though he were going out of the room; but his wife laid her hand on his arm.

'Do not speak to her before the children,' she said, in her low, quiet voice. 'I will go up and question her.'

'No! I must speak to her. You must know,' said he, turning to his uncle and aunt, 'my missus has an old servant, as faithful as ever woman was, I do believe, as far as love goes, – but at the same time, who does not speak truth, as even the missus must allow. Now, my notion is, that this Norah of ours has been come over by some good-for-nothing chap (for she's at the time o' life when they say women pray for husbands – "any, good Lord, any") and has let him into our house, and the chap has made off with your brooch, and m'appen many another thing beside. It's only saying that Norah is soft-hearted and doesn't stick at a white lie – that's all, missus.'

It was curious to notice how his tone, his eyes, his whole face was changed, as he spoke to his wife; but he was the resolute man through all. She knew better than to oppose him; so she went upstairs, and told Norah that her master wanted to speak to her, and that she would take care of the children in the meanwhile.

Norah rose to go, without a word. Her thoughts were these:

'If they tear me to pieces, they shall never know through me. He may come – and then, just Lord have mercy upon us all! for some of us are dead folk to a certainty. But *he* shall do it; not me.'

You may fancy, now, her look of determination, as she faced her master alone in the dining-room; Mr and Mrs Chadwick having left the affair in their nephew's hands, seeing that he took it up with such vehemence.

'Norah! Who was that man that came to my house last night?'

'Man, sir!' As if infinitely surprised; but it was only to gain time.

'Yes; the man that Mary let in; that she went upstairs to the nursery to tell you about; that you came down to speak to; the same chap, I make no doubt, that you took into the nursery to have your talk out with; the one Ailsie saw, and afterwards dreamed about; thinking, poor wench! she saw him say his prayers, when nothing, I'll be bound, was further from his thoughts; the one that took Mrs Chadwick's brooch, value ten pounds. Now, Norah! Don't go off. I'm as sure as my name's Thomas Openshaw that you knew nothing of this robbery. But I do think you've been imposed on, and that's the truth. Some good-for-nothing chap has been making up to you, and you've been just like all other women, and have turned a soft place in your heart to him; and he came last night a-lovyering, and you had him up in the nursery, and he made use of his opportunities, and made off with a few things on his way down! Come, now, Norah; it's no blame to you, only you must not be such a fool again! Tell us,' he continued, 'what name he gave you, Norah. I'll be bound, it was not the right one; but it will be a clue for the police.'

Norah drew herself up. 'You may ask that question, and taunt me with my being single, and with my credulity, as you will, Master Openshaw. You'll get no answer from me. As for the brooch, and the story of theft and burglary; if any friend ever came to see me (which I defy you to prove, and deny), he'd be just as much above doing such a thing as you yourself, Mr Openshaw – and more so, too; for I'm not at all sure as everything you have is rightly come by, or would be yours long, if every man had his own.' She meant, of course, his wife; but he understood her to refer to his property in goods and chattels.

'Now, my good woman,' said he, 'I'll just tell you truly, I never trusted you out and out; but my wife liked you, and I thought you had many a good point about you. If you once begin to sauce me, I'll have the police to you, and get out the truth in a court of justice, if you'll not tell it me quietly and civilly here. Now, the best thing you can do is quietly to tell me who the fellow is. Look here! a man comes to my house; asks for you; you take him upstairs; a valuable brooch is missing next day; we know that you, and Mary, and cook, are honest; but you refuse to tell us who the

man is. Indeed, you've told me one lie already about him, saying
no one was here last night. Now, I just put it to you, what do you
think a policeman would say to this, or a magistrate? A magistrate
would soon make you tell the truth, my good woman.'

'There's never the creature born that should get it out of me,'
said Norah. 'Not unless I choose to tell.'

'I've a great mind to see,' said Mr Openshaw, growing angry at
the defiance. Then, checking himself, he thought before he spoke
again:

'Norah, for your missus' sake I don't want to go to extremities.
Be a sensible woman, if you can. It's no great disgrace, after all, to
have been taken in. I ask you once more – as a friend – who was
this man that you let into my house last night?'

No answer. He repeated the question in an impatient tone. Still
no answer. Norah's lips were set in determination not to speak.

'Then there is but one thing to be done. I shall send for a
policeman.'

'You will not,' said Norah, starting forward. 'You shall not, sir!
No policeman shall touch me. I know nothing of the brooch, but I
know this: ever since I was four-and-twenty, I have thought more
of your wife than of myself: ever since I saw her, a poor mother-
less girl, put upon in her uncle's house, I have thought more of
serving her than of serving myself! I have cared for her and her
child, as nobody ever cared for me. I don't cast blame on you, sir,
but I say it's ill giving up one's life to any one; for, at the end, they
will turn round upon you, and forsake you. Why does not my
missus come herself to suspect me? Maybe, she is gone for the
police? But I don't stay here, either for police, or magistrate, or
master. You're an unlucky lot. I believe there's a curse on you. I'll
leave you this very day. Yes! I'll leave that poor Ailsie, too. I will!
No good ever will come to you!'

Mr Openshaw was utterly astonished at this speech; most of
which was completely unintelligible to him, as may easily be
supposed. Before he could make up his mind what to say, or what
to do, Norah had left the room. I do not think he had ever really
intended to send for the police to this old servant of his wife's; for
he had never for a moment doubted her perfect honesty. But he
had intended to compel her to tell him who the man was, and in
this he was baffled. He was, consequently, much irritated. He
returned to his uncle and aunt in a state of great annoyance and
perplexity, and told them he could get nothing out of the woman;

that some man had been in the house the night before; but that she refused to tell who he was. At this moment his wife came in, greatly agitated, and asked what had happened to Norah; for that she had put on her things in passionate haste, and left the house.

'This looks suspicious,' said Mr Chadwick. 'It is not the way in which an honest person would have acted.'

Mr Openshaw kept silence. He was sorely perplexed. But Mrs Openshaw turned round on Mr Chadwick, with a sudden fierceness no one ever saw in her before.

'You don't know Norah, uncle! She is gone because she is deeply hurt at being suspected. Oh, I wish I had seen her – that I had spoken to her myself. She would have told me anything.' Alice wrung her hands.

'I must confess,' continued Mr Chadwick to his nephew, in a lower voice, 'I can't make you out. You used to be a word and a blow, and oftenest the blow first; and now, when there is every cause for suspicion, you just do nought. Your missus is a very good woman, I grant; but she may have been put upon as well as other folk, I suppose. If you don't send for the police, I shall.'

'Very well,' replied Mr Openshaw, surlily. 'I can't clear Norah. She won't clear herself, as I believe she might if she would. Only I wash my hands of it; for I am sure the woman herself is honest, and she's lived a long time with my wife, and I don't like her to come to shame.'

'But she will then be forced to clear herself. That, at any rate, will be a good thing.'

'Very well, very well! I am heart-sick of the whole business. Come, Alice, come up to the babies; they'll be in a sore way. I tell you, uncle,' he said, turning round once more to Mr Chadwick, suddenly and sharply, after his eye had fallen on Alice's wan, tearful, anxious face, 'I'll have no sending for the police, after all. I'll buy my aunt twice as handsome a brooch this very day; but I'll not have Norah suspected, and my missus plagued. There's for you!'

He and his wife left the room. Mr Chadwick quietly waited till he was out of hearing, and then said to his wife, 'For all Tom's heroics, I'm just quietly going for a detective, wench. Thou need'st know nought about it.'

He went to the police-station and made a statement of the case. He was gratified by the impression which the evidence against Norah seemed to make. The men all agreed in his opinion, and steps were to be immediately taken to find out where she was. Most probably, as they suggested, she had gone at once to the man, who, to all appearance, was her lover. When Mr Chadwick asked how they would find her out, they smiled, shook their heads, and spoke of mysterious but infallible ways and means. He returned to his nephew's house with a very comfortable opinion of his own sagacity. He was met by his wife with a penitent face.

'Oh, master, I've found my brooch! It was just sticking by its pin in the flounce of my brown silk, that I wore yesterday. I took it off in a hurry, and it must have caught in it; and I hung up my gown in the closet. Just now, when I was going to fold it up, there was the brooch! I am very vexed, but I never dreamt but what it was lost!'

Her husband, muttering something very like 'Confound thee and thy brooch too! I wish I'd never given it thee,' snatched up his hat, and rushed back to the station, hoping to be in time to stop the police from searching for Norah. But a detective was already gone off on the errand.

Where was Norah? Half mad with the strain of the fearful secret, she had hardly slept through the night for thinking what must be done. Upon this terrible state of mind had come Ailsie's questions, showing that she had seen the Man, as the unconscious child called her father. Lastly came the suspicion of her honesty. She was little less than crazy as she ran upstairs and dashed on her bonnet and shawl; leaving all else, even her purse, behind her. In that house she would not stay. That was all she knew or was clear about. She would not even see the children again, for fear it should weaken her. She dreaded above everything Mr Frank's return to claim his wife. She could not tell what remedy there was for a sorrow so tremendous, for her to stay to witness. The desire of escaping from the coming event was a stronger motive for her departure, than her soreness about the suspicions directed against her; although this last had been the final goad to the course she took. She walked away almost at headlong speed; sobbing as she went, as she had not dared to do during the past night for fear of exciting wonder in those who might hear her. Then she stopped. An idea came into her mind that she would leave London altogether, and betake herself to her native town of Liverpool. She felt in her pocket for her purse as she drew near the Euston Square station with this intention. She had left it at home. Her poor head aching, her eyes swollen with crying, she had to stand still, and think, as well as she could, where next she should bend her steps. Suddenly the thought flashed into her mind that she would go and find out poor Mr Frank. She had been hardly kind to him the night before, though her heart had bled for him ever since. She remembered his telling her, when she inquired for his address, almost as she had pushed him out of the door, of some hotel in a street not far distant from Euston Square. Thither she went: with what intention she scarcely knew, but to assuage her conscience by telling him how much she pitied him. In her present state she felt herself unfit to counsel, or restrain, or assist, or do aught else but sympathize and weep. The people of the inn said such a person had been there; had arrived only the day before; had gone out soon after arrival, leaving his luggage in their care; but had never come back. Norah asked for leave to sit down, and await the gentleman's return. The landlady – pretty secure in the deposit of luggage against any probable injury – showed her into a room, and quietly locked the door on the outside. Norah was utterly worn out, and fell asleep – a shivering, starting, uneasy slumber, which lasted for hours.

The detective, meanwhile, had come up with her some time before she entered the hotel, into which he followed her. Asking the landlady to detain her for an hour or so, without giving any reason beyond showing his authority (which made the landlady applaud herself a good deal for having locked her in), he went back to the police-station to report his proceedings. He could have taken her directly; but his object was, if possible, to trace out the man who was supposed to have committed the robbery. Then he heard of the discovery of the brooch; and consequently did not care to return.

Norah slept till even the summer evening began to close in. Then started up. Some one was at the door. It would be Mr Frank; and she dizzily pushed back her ruffled grey hair, which had fallen over her eyes, and stood looking to see him. Instead, there came in Mr Openshaw and a policeman.

'This is Norah Kennedy,' said Mr Openshaw.

'Oh, sir,' said Norah, 'I did not touch the brooch; indeed I did not. Oh, sir, I cannot live to be thought so badly of'; and very sick and faint, she suddenly sank down on the ground. To her surprise, Mr Openshaw raised her up very tenderly. Even the policeman helped to lay her on the sofa; and, at Mr Openshaw's desire, he went for some wine and sandwiches; for the poor gaunt woman lay there almost as if dead with weariness and exhaustion.

'Norah,' said Mr Openshaw, in his kindest voice, 'the brooch is found. It was hanging to Mrs Chadwick's gown. I beg your pardon. Most truly I beg your pardon, for having troubled you about it. My wife is almost broken-hearted. Eat, Norah – or, stay, first drink this glass of wine,' said he, lifting her head, and pouring a little down her throat.

As she drank, she remembered where she was, and who she was waiting for. She suddenly pushed Mr Openshaw away, saying, 'Oh, sir, you must go. You must not stop a minute. If he comes back, he will kill you.'

'Alas, Norah! I do not know who "he" is. But some one is gone away who will never come back: some one who knew you, and whom I am afraid you cared for.'

'I don't understand you, sir,' said Norah, her master's kind and sorrowful manner bewildering her yet more than his words. The policeman had left the room at Mr Openshaw's desire, and they two were alone.

'You know what I mean, when I say some one is gone who will never come back. I mean that he is dead!'

'Who?' said Norah, trembling all over.

'A poor man has been found in the Thames this morning – drowned.'

'Did he drown himself?' asked Norah, solemnly.

'God only knows,' replied Mr Openshaw, in the same tone. 'Your name and address at our house were found in his pocket; that, and his purse, were the only things that were found upon him. I am sorry to say it, my poor Norah; but you are required to go and identify him.'

'To what?' asked Norah.

'To say who it is. It is always done, in order that some reason may be discovered for the suicide – if suicide it was. I make no doubt, he was the man who came to see you at our house last night. It is very sad, I know.' He made pauses between each little clause, in order to try and bring back her senses, which he feared were wandering – so wild and sad was her look.

'Master Openshaw,' said she, at last, 'I've a dreadful secret to tell you – only you must never breathe it to any one, and you and I must hide it away for ever. I thought to have done it all by myself, but I see I cannot. Yon poor man – yes! the dead, drowned creature is, I fear, Mr Frank, my mistress's first husband!'

Mr Openshaw sat down, as if shot. He did not speak; but, after a while, he signed to Norah to go on.

'He came to me the other night, when – God be thanked! – you were all away at Richmond. He asked me if his wife was dead or alive. I was a brute, and thought more of your all coming home than of his sore trial; I spoke out sharp, and said she was married again, and very content and happy. I all but turned him away: and now he lies dead and cold.'

'God forgive me!' said Mr Openshaw.

'God forgive us all!' said Norah. 'Yon poor man needs forgiveness, perhaps, less than any one among us. He had been among the savages – shipwrecked – I know not what – and he had written letters which had never reached my poor missus.'

'He saw his child!'

'He saw her – yes! I took him up, to give his thoughts another start; for I believed he was going mad on my hands. I came to seek him here, as I more than half promised. My mind misgave me when I heard he never came in. Oh, sir, it must be him!'

Mr Openshaw rang the bell. Norah was almost too much stunned to wonder at what he did. He asked for writing materials, wrote a letter, and then said to Norah:

'I am writing to Alice, to say I shall be unavoidably absent for a few days; that I have found you; that you are well, and send her your love, and will come home to-morrow. You must go with me to the police court; you must identify the body; I will pay high to keep names and details out of the papers.'

'But where are you going, sir?'

He did not answer her directly. Then he said:

'Norah! I must go with you, and look on the face of the man whom I have so injured – unwittingly, it is true; but it seems to me as if I had killed him. I will lay his head in the grave as if he were my only brother: and how he must have hated me! I cannot go home to my wife till all that I can do for him is done. Then I go with a dreadful secret on my mind. I shall never speak of it again, after these days are over. I know you will not, either.' He shook hands with her; and they never named the subject again, the one to the other.

Norah went home to Alice the next day. Not a word was said on the cause of her abrupt departure a day or two before. Alice had been charged by her husband, in his letter, not to allude to the supposed theft of the brooch; so she, implicitly obedient to those whom she loved both by nature and habit, was entirely silent on the subject, only treated Norah with the most tender respect, as if to make up for unjust suspicion.

Nor did Alice inquire into the reason why Mr Openshaw had been absent during his uncle and aunt's visit, after he had once said that it was unavoidable. He came back grave and quiet; and from that time forth was curiously changed. More thoughtful, and perhaps less active; quite as decided in conduct, but with new and different rules for the guidance of that conduct. Towards Alice he could hardly be more kind than he had always been; but he now seemed to look upon her as some one sacred, and to be treated with reverence, as well as tenderness. He throve in business, and made a large fortune, one half of which was settled upon her.

Long years after these events – a few months after her mother died – Ailsie and her 'father' (as she always called Mr Openshaw) drove to a cemetery a little way out of town, and she was carried to a certain mound by her maid, who was then sent back to the carriage. There was a headstone, with F. W. and a date upon it. That was all. Sitting by the grave, Mr Openshaw told her the story; and for the sad fate of that poor father whom she had never seen, he shed the only tears she ever saw fall from his eyes.